The Novelization

RICHARD CURTIS

based on an original screenplay by
JEFF LIEBERMAN

Encyclopocalypse Publications
www.encyclopocalypse.com

The Novelization

Prologue

It was a sultry night in July of 1960. For four straight days the white sun had baked Long County on the east coast of Georgia until the rich black loam became almost concrete-hard, the crops drooped like troops of parched soldiers, and the air seared the lungs of those brave or foolish enough to venture out in it. And at night there was scarcely any respite. The sea breeze that normally drifted in from Sapelo Sound at dusk seemed reluctant to challenge the solid wall of stagnant hot air lying over the shore, and half-heartedly rippled through a fringe of moss-festooned live-oaks before faltering and finally dying.

Little Roger Grimes, age seven-and-a-half years old, lay atop his sweat-damp bed, clad only in a rough linen nightshirt that his mother had cut down from one of his daddy's worn-out workshirts. He probably could have slept naked, but the shirt reminded him of his mama, now dead two years, and it comforted him, protected him like armor against the scary thoughts that had lately begun to obsess him.

Thoughts about—worms.

Having grown up on his daddy's bait farm, Roger should have been able to take worms for granted by now, should have been able to regard them the way, say, his friend Bobby Brinton regarded the manure on *his* daddy's cattle farm. After a while, Bobby had told him, you could walk through the stuff up to your ankles, even eat a sandwich while working in it, and you wouldn't even smell it, wouldn't even know it was there, really.

Same way with worms. Until his mother had died, God rest her soul, of influenza complicated by fatal double pneumonia, Roger had thought of worms the same way he thought of the air he breathed or the soil he trod on or the rain that trickled over his face. Worms were just part of his environment. Worms were the medium in which he existed. Worms were the way his daddy made his living, a commodity like cotton or soybeans, a currency like coins or paper money. Though the city people who came to Fly Creek to fish sometimes shuddered at the sight of a six-inch sandworm writhing on a hook, or the touch of a dozen of them, like so many greasy segmented rubber tubes, responding to a hand thrust into the bait-box, Roger was scarcely aware that these creatures were any different from a pet cat or dog. Hell, he'd once seen this lady, a wife of a Savannah businessman come to Fly Creek to try his hand at the fabled bass that haunted these estuarial waters, faint dead away when Roger reached into a crateful of sandworms right up to his shoulder. After that he tried to remember that most folks didn't regard worms quite the same way he did.

At any rate, that had been his attitude till his mama died. Then something happened at her funeral, and he'd never been able to look at a worm again without feeling a wave of nausea in the pit of his stomach. His mama's casket, a plain pine box that his daddy had lovingly hewn out of some loblolly timber on their farm, rested on a little wooden platform above the yawning hole into which it would soon be lowered. It had been drizzling, and now it began to pour in earnest. Clutching his daddy's hand tightly, Roger leaned forward to stare with curiosity into the grave.

As he looked, rivulets of water trickled over the rim of the grave and washed dirt and clay into the hole reflexively, his eyes accustomed to seeking them in rain-soaked soil, Roger noticed the shiny purplish heads of earthworms, disturbed by the trickling rainwater, poking out of the fractured walls. Suddenly, his grief, which Lord only knows was unbearable enough, was suffused with horror as he realized that in due time the box in which his mother's body resided would rot and be invaded by those very worms—no, not just the box, but her body itself.

At that moment Preacher Borden, the purple-faced minister from Fly Creek First Baptist, raised his voice over the splatter of torrential rain on the muddy cemetery grounds, and read a familiar passage from the Book of Job, Chapter xix, verse 25:

"I know that my redeemer liveth," he shouted hoarsely, "and that he shall stand at the later day upon the earth. And though after my skin worms destroy this body, yet in my flesh shall I see God."

Roger's eyes widened and the black eyeballs bulged like two rounded chunks of anthracite. His body began to tremble and his fists clenched involuntarily. "No!" he screamed. "NO, NO, NOT WORMS, NOT MY POOR MAMA!" His father clutched at the boy's wrist but Roger yanked away, sobbing hysterically, the rainwater spilling down his ebony locks and mingling with his tears. "DON'T LET THE WORMS EAT HER, PLEASE! DON'T LET THE WORMS GET MY MAMA!"

The poor distracted boy leaped into the grave and began pounding the walls with his fists, pulping the soft heads of the earthworms they ventured out of their sodden abodes. Roger's daddy and two strong farmhands had leaped into the grave and hauled Roger out, and one of the hands hustled the boy to a car while the shockstricken preacher, congregation, and the bereaved husband finished the ceremony in triple-time.

Still insane with grief and fear, Roger refused to return to the bait farm. His daddy had to put him up with his cousins in town until, no less than three weeks later, the boy returned to his senses and came back to the farm.

Though the incident was eventually submerged in the minds of Willie Grimes and his son Roger, Roger could never quite look at, touch, or even think about worms the way he had before his mother's death. He could scarcely bring himself to visit his mother's grave, and now when he worked with worms on the farm it was with ill-disguised repugnance. He had dreams so ghastly it was a blessing he forgot them the next morning—except for one recurring one he could not forget, a dream that he himself was a worm, a huge sandworm three feet long, comfortably ensconced in the soil where the world and the bright light of the sun couldn't find him until one day his father thrust a spade into the ground and found him and grasped him by the neck and yanked him out of the' earth, thrusting him into a sack with a thousand others like him. Then one day his daddy pulled him out of the sack and impaled his belly with a fishhook....

Now, on this sultry night in July of 1960, the restless boy sat up and thrust his long legs over ·the side of the bed. The broiling night smothered him like a blanket and he stuck his head out of the window, sucking air into his mouth in the foolish hope of catching some errant pocket of coolness. No such luck.

He looked up at the moon, a football-shaped blue-white jewel hanging high on the throat of the night, and though the sight of this lovely satellite inspired romantic or philosophical or inspirational thoughts in the minds of just about any other soul who happened to look at *it* that night, to Roger it said only one thing: *There would be no worms tonight.*

For, light is the enemy of the worm. Not just the brilliant sun, but even the subdued moon, indeed even a flicker of heat lightning on an otherwise black night, is enough to keep a worm from surfacing. In the obsessive mind of Roger Grimes, where everything had begun to have associations with worms, a moonlit night meant that his enemies remained underground where they would give him a few hours' surcease from tortured thoughts and dreams.

Then he noticed another light—no, two.

One was the glow of an electric globe filtering through the window and cracks of the small clapboard outbuilding, formerly tenanted by chickens, where his father crated and stored his worms. In the southwest corner of this building, his father had created a little area for himself which he alternately referred to as his office, laboratory, or library. There, when the day's work was done, Willie Grimes repaired to read about, examine, and experiment with his worms, an occupation which Roger found almost beyond belief. It was bad enough his father worked with the creatures all day long; it was incomprehensible that the man should work with them at day's end too, when any other laboring man in his right mind settled before the television set to watch a baseball game, or drove into town to hoist a beer with the boys or seek the companionship of a woman. But then Roger correctly wondered whether his father was indeed quite in his right mind.

Had the yellow glow of the unshaded lightbulb in his father's office been the only light coming from the building, Roger probably would have pulled his head in and tried to wrestle with sleep again in his bed. But after a moment he saw a brilliant blue flash as well. It lasted only a second, but it was so strong it left its imprint on his retina for a whole minute afterwards. A couple of minutes later, it happened again. It reminded him of the unbearably bright blue sparkle of an acetylene torch on steel, except that the source was probably not gas but electricity. Roger was able to conclude this because he'd noticed the yellow light in the office dim almost to extinction where the blue light blazed, meaning the blue light was draining electricity substantially.

Though normally apprehensive about visiting his daddy's office, even at a reasonable daytime hour let alone the cusp of midnight, Roger's curiosity propelled him to the slat-back chair in his room where his trousers were. He stepped into them hurriedly, hitched the straps to the studs at the waist, and stepped into his heavy work boots. He clomped down the steps of the farmhouse, the tails of his nightshirt fluttering behind him, and through the screen door. down the porch steps, and across the twenty-five yards of dirt path to the outbuilding. As he was halfway there, the blue spark illuminated the building and its environs magically. casting the surrounding trees into azure-limned silhouettes and hurling grotesque blue shadows across the expanse of tilled soil where the worms were farmed.

"Daddy?" Roger decided to call out as he approached the outbuilding so as not to scare his father.

"Son? That you? Come in. come in! See what we got here."

Roger stepped on the split log that served as a step up to the door, then shouldered his way apprehensively into the building. The office was small, about ten by ten, with the low ceiling typical of chicken coops, which Willie Grimes always complained about but never got around to doing anything about. On the wall opposite the door Willie had erected some simple pine shelves that sagged in the middle, like a swayback mule, beneath the weight of dozens and dozens of heavy volumes. Willie Grimes was self-educated and had trouble reading the Savannah newspapers, but when it came to any literature pertaining to worms, he not only grasped it but seemed to grasp beyond it, to Latin terms, to physiological structure, to cell composition. to the intricacies of the nervous and vascular and digestive and reproductive systems. Never in a rush, he might spend several nights in a row hunting down the exact meaning of the term *podial papilla* or fitting some family member like *Scalibregma* into its class, *Polychaeta*, and that into its phylum, *Annelida*. He had the amateur's passion, determination, curiosity, and patience, and had he had a formal education might well have made important contributions to the story of these creatures.

Roger stared for a moment at the books piled on bis father's shelves: "The Physiology of the Vascular System of Invertebrates," "Properties of the Nervous Systems of Annelids," "Catalogue of the Polychaetous Annelids of the World," and on and on. Even a few books in foreign languages, which the man had brought to doctors and teachers and other professional people in the community well versed in those languages, and prevailed on them to translate passages for him.

On the wall to his left stood an old kitchen table that his father had converted into an experimental station, with trays of dyes, chemicals, and bottles and beakers of multi-colored solutions too exotic for Roger to begin to figure out. On the wall to his right was a crate of worms about the size of an orange crate but with slats fitted tightly together unlike an orange crate. His father was hunched over it sorting out a tangle of sandworms.

Roger sniffed the air and inhaled the familiar odors of freshly turned loam, the ammoniac stench of worm excreta. the variety of chemical smells mingling disagreeably, and yet another smell, one which he had difficulty identifying though he had smelled it before. It was something he had sniffed— where?—yes, down by the high-voltage electric towers after a rainstorm. He had no name for it, but as if reading his mind, his daddy. without looking up, said, "That's called ozone, boy."

"Ozone?"

"Uh-huh. You get it when an electrical spark jumps through the atmosphere. I don't know exactly how it works, but it's like it burns up some of the air and causes it to stink somewhat."

Willie Grimes straightened up and looked a little crossly at his son. He was a rough-hewn man with straight jet hair and dark, humorless eyes. His shoulders were rounded from the double burden of farming and hunching over books and laboratory apparatus, and his face was stubbled with the salt-and-pepper of a prematurely graying beard. Willie Grimes was thirty-eight but he looked close to fifty.

"Am I bothering you, daddy?"

"No. no. Just shut the door before every moth in the county flies in."

Roger stepped into the room and closed the wooden door behind him. His father had just draped a sandworm over the back of his fist and now carried it to the table. He deposited it in the soil that filled an old fishtank and pulled the lightbulb that hung from the ceiling close to the creature. It bunched its segmented body together like an accordion, plunged its head into the soil, convulsed and squirmed for some thirty seconds, then disappeared entirely, drawing its quivering tail into the dirt behind it. Then he reached behind the fishtank and grasped two wires, a red and a black, tipped with alligator clips at one end and plugged into a socket at the other. He made sure not to touch the clips together. Roger realized that the blue flashes were connected with these electric wires somehow and gazed with fascination at his father's hands.

Grimes turned his back on his son and tried to settle down to his experiment, but after a moment, as if feeling the boy's eyes boring into his spine, he put the wires down carefully on a wooden block and turned around to face Roger, a scowl reddening his cheeks. "Something bothering you, boy?"

"I just couldn't sleep. It's hot as an oven in there, daddy."

"Well, what can I do about it?"

"Nothin'. I just thought I'd come by and see what you're doin'. Saw the blue sparks comin' from your window."

His father tilted his head and looked gimlet-eyed at his son. "You don't want to hear about it."

"Oh, I don't mind."

"I know how you are about..." He clipped off the sentence and simply gestured in the direction of the worm crate.

"I said I don't mind, daddy," Roger said. It wasn't really true, but the boy had no way of conveying that he'd rather be with his daddy in this creepy room than alone with his fears in the house.

Willie Grimes ran a knuckle over his stubbly cheeks. "I'm testing the effects of electric current on these here worms," he said, tapping a talon-like fingernail on the glass of the dirt-filled fishtank.

"What's it supposed to do?" the boy asked, taking a step closer but keeping his distance respectfully.

His father thrust his chin in the direction of a scientific journal propped up delicately against an empty beaker on the corner of the table. "S'posed to stimulate 'em."

"Stimulate 'em to do what, exactly?"

"I don't know about sandworms," Grimes replied. "The experiment in this journal was done on a different kind of worm, a tubeworm known as…" He wrapped his lips around the Latin term, then shrugged. "Well, what the hell's the difference what it's called? Anyway, they ran a current through the saline solution this worm was swimming in. Doubled its length in half the time it usually takes, meaning it consumed its food at twice the usual rate. Don't ask me why—just did."

"What do you think it'll do for a sandworm? I mean, shootin' a current through it?"

Grimes turned his palms up. "I'm not sure, but I'll tell you one thing it does."

"What's that?"

"Brings 'em to the surface like they been goosed." His mouth turned up in the closest thing to a smile that Willie Grimes was capable of.

"In spite of the light, you mean?" the boy asked, inching closer to the table.

"Uh-huh. Of course, soon as I stopped applying the juice, they burrowed home right away, but for the moment at least they lost their fear of light."

Roger peered into the fishtank, then into the black depths of his father's eyes. They gleamed unnaturally, like those of a hunter scenting a kill.

"You don't grasp what that means, do you, boy?" Grimes

said, shaking his head at the timid, disappointing kid who stood tentatively before him, body tensed as if prepared to leap out the door the moment something un expected happened. like a wary fox approaching a baited trap.

"What you afraid of, boy?" he snapped. "Jesus, you work with me all day long shoveling thousands of these things out of the ground. So why should you be afraid now?"

Roger shrank from his father but avoided the question, choosing instead to answer it with a question of his own. "Why do you do this, daddy? Why can't you be like other daddies? Preston Tinker, *his* daddy took him to the county fair the other n—"

Grimes smacked his fist into his palm. "I don't give a fiddler's finger what Preston Tinker's daddy does, or anybody else's! This is the only thing that interests me. Sure I know what some people say about me, that I'm wormhappy and gone off the deep end. Well, that don't bother me none. Those are the kind of people who've never looked beneath the surface of things, who think a worm's just a worm. Why, there's so many kinds of worms nobody's counted 'em all up yet. There's earthworms, flat worms, marine worms, horsehair worms, flukes, leeches, roundworms, tapeworms, and hundreds, maybe thousands of species within each of those classifications."

Roger held up his hands. He'd heard his father's speech before, a long diatribe the man always hauled out whenever scoffers put him on the defensive, and it was the last thing Roger wanted to hear tonight. All he'd come out here for was the human companionship. He just wanted his daddy to tell him it was all right, no need to be afraid of the dark. I love you son, ain't nobody gonna harm you, maybe tomorrow *I'll* take you to the fair too. Instead, Willie Grimes had gotten wound up on his endless oration on the subject of worms.

"…they cut open a worm, all they see is its guts. Guts, hah! Why, you dissect a worm, you'll find as many organs as you II find if you cut up a human being, and some of 'em just as sophisticated. Look at these eyes I've collected..."

He rapped a sealed preserves jar with a horny knuckle. Roger glanced at it long enough to see hundreds of tiny eyeballs floating languidly in formaldehyde. He felt his gorge rising and cut his father off with a sharp chop of the hand in the air. "I'm sorry I asked, daddy."

His father was not completely insensitive. He lowered his eyes, reached into his overalls, pulled out a soil crusted red handkerchief, and mopped his forehead. *"I'm* sorry. I keep thinkin' other folks are as interested in this stuff as I am. Look how I've worked up a sweat." He reached out and placed a tender hand on the boy's shoulder. "Whyn't you get to bed, sonny?"

The moments of warmth between father and son were so rare, Roger reveled in this one and wanted to prolong it. He knew that the easiest way to do this was to express interest in his father's work. "What about the electricity, daddy?"

"Huh?"

"You started to say somethin' about the importance of this electricity business."

Willie looked skeptically at his boy from under heavy black brows. "You don't really care, do you?"

"I asked, didn't I?"

Willie shrugged. then an odd expression came into his face, one that Roger had rarely seen. It was a combination of craftiness and greed, and it was terribly discomfiting, like the face of a wizard, Roger thought, who has discovered a way to convert lead into gold. Willie's eyes glowed and his lips parted in a grimace that seemed to confirm the madness of which his neighbors all suspected him.

"You know how much work we got to do to farm worms now, right?",

Roger closed his eyes and pictured the backbreaking toil to

which his father, being too poor to afford help, had subjected the boy from the day he was old enough to know which end of a spade goes into the soil. "Sure."

"Well, suppose we could bring the worms to the surface without all that labor? Suppose," he said, illustrating by bringing his two index fingers together like the ends of two electrical cables, "we could apply a electrical current—I mean a *real* heavy dose, not just your everyday household current—directly to the soil. Not just to a fishtank full of worms, like here, but to five or ten acres at a time. Hah? You see, boy? Hah?" Grimes began sweating again and his chest heaved with excitement.

Roger closed his eyes a moment and seemed able to read the image in his father's mind as if it were being projected onto the screen in his own.

"That's right!" his father panted "You could harvest those sumbitches like so many string beans. We could do a day's work in two hours and have eight hours to spare. We could be rich, boy! Rich! Come here. Come on, come on, come on," he said feverishly. churning the air with his hand.

As if spellbound by his father's vision, Roger stepped up to the table.

"Now, pick up those two wires, careful not to let the tips touch. That's right. Now, stick the points into the soil here in the fishtank, about six inches apart. Soil is damp, see, so you're gonna get a current. Don't worry, you ain't gonna get electrocuted. There."

The clips sparked blue as they entered the damp dirt, sending wisps of smoke and an acrid odor of ozone curling under the boy's nostrils. The yellow bulb overhead dimmed and flickered, making his father's face as the man leaned over the fishtank, appear ghastly and un natural. In fact, Roger found the sight of his father's face compellingly fascinating. It was indeed the face of a wizard, flickering blue and yellow in "the quavering light, tobacco-stained teeth bared in a mad smile, dark eyes, bulging out of their sockets, breath coming in short, evil-smelling gusts.

Suddenly his father's face darkened. "Watch what you're about, boy!"

"Huh?"

Roger looked down and started to withdraw his hand from the fishtank, but it was too late. At least half a dozen sandworms had burst out of their refuge in the dirt, like missiles popping out of their silos, and one of them had grasped Roger by the meat of his thumb.

The mouth of the sandworm contains a pair of sharp needle-like fangs, and Roger had been scratched or bitten by them so often he was practically insensitive to them. They were no more painful than the thrust of a mosquito's proboscis, and a worm that fastened to one's flesh was easily shaken loose with a flick of the hand.

Roger flicked his hand, and suddenly a pain shot down his thumb and up his arm such as he'd never in his life experienced. He looked at his thumb and the worm had not merely fixed on to the flesh like a leech but had bored through it like an auger bit and was now pulling its segmented anterior behind it into the meat of his thumb. Roger shrieked with pain and horror and beat his thumb against the glass wall of the fish tank, squashing the body of the worm in a splatter of blood and slime. But the head and about an inch of the worm's body had still penetrated inside his thumb and continued boring their way inside. "Daddy, do something, do something, please!" the boy screamed hysterically. "It's killing me, it's killing me!"

His father held his wrist in a vise-like grip, staring in mute helplessness as the worm burrowed beneath the flesh. For what seemed like minutes the man was paralyzed with a mixture of scientific interest and fright. Then he twisted his head, casting around the room for an implement.

He found one. A scalpel.

The boy's eyes widened with yet more horror. "Daddy. Now what are you gonna do?"

"Hold still, boy."

"Daddy, no."

"Hold still, I said!"

"Daddy, *Daddy!* DADDY…!"

Chapter One

Willie Grimes' bait farm hadn't changed very much in the fifteen years since that traumatic night. Willie had aged, it seemed, two years for every chronological one and was now a gray-haired, round-shouldered, dour man given to cruel outbursts of temper. Roger had survived that incident with a rather brutal scar to show for it, but an even more brutal scar on his soul where no one could see it. He was a strapping lad, handsome with an abundance of black hair and soft cow-eyes. He still worked for his father, but there had been no more experiments from that night to the present.

The rest of the town of Fly Creek hadn't changed much either. Andy's Barber Shop was still there, its proprietor now an object of humorous derision for having lost most of his hair. Betsy's Luncheonette had changed hands and was now owned by Millie, a buxom orange-haired woman fairly bursting out of her pink rayon waitress uniform. There were a few new gas stations, the courthouse had gotten a new flagpole, and the church a new coat of paint. Willie Grimes had hung a new sign in front of his bait shop but otherwise it was the same hole-in-the-wall squeezed between two other shops. Unless you were going fishing in Fly Lake or in the coastal waters around Sapelo Sound, you'd pass Willie's shop and not even know it was there.

Tonight, that sign swung violently in the teeth of the fiercest storm the town had experienced in no one was sure how long. Oh, there'd been hurricanes, but Fly Creek had been lucky never to catch one squarely. This wasn't a hurricane, but an odd confrontation of low and high-pressure fronts that had worked up gusts of wind well over a hundred miles per hour. Buster Martin, not liking the sound or looks of it, had closed his tavern early and sent his patrons home to sit by their windows shaking their heads as the wind swept tree branches horizontal to the ground, bent saplings to low angles or tore them out of the ground by their roots altogether, yanked rotten tree limbs out of their sockets and flung them against buildings and cars.

The rain drummed maddeningly on rooftops, thundered down on pavements, made morasses out of lawns and even tore gulleys out of fields and farmland heavily planted with grasses and crops. Down at the inlet between town and Sapelo Sound, half the rowboats and mall fishing vessels had either been driven together in a crunch of wooden planking or foundered with rainwater up to the gunwales. Lightning in jagged blue forks thrust angrily at trees, utility poles, lightning rods and television aerials, and on a few occasions the children huddling in their homes, taught to count the seconds between lightning flash and thunderclap (every second counting for eleven hundred feet of comfort and safety), found the two occurring all but simultaneously and hurled themselves into their parents' arms, sobbing.

Were it not for an ominous occurrence on a hill behind the town, Fly Creek would have weathered the storm with little but average damage. But on that hill stood Tower #4511, a high-voltage tower carrying two hundred thousand volts of electricity from Sapelo Sound Station to the rural townships along the coast, including Fly Creek. Torrents of rainwater sluiced down Chickering's Hill and lapped around the cement foundation of the steel tower, undermining it and exposing the platform supporting the heavy legs and girders. For a moment the rain mysteriously abated, but an instant later it hurled itself with even deadlier fury at he exposed tower. It swayed, tugging fretfully at the lines that carried the juice from the Georgia Power & Light booster station a mile or two to the north. and played havoc with the cable that carried current off to the Fly Creek transformer station.

The citizens of Fly Creek noted the dimming of their lights apprehensively, but without alarm. Lines do, go down in heavy storms, but after a few hours of inconvenience the utility people locate the problem and restore power. Thus when the lights flickered one last time, then went out for good, there were many groans and sighs of resignation but nothing more.

The lights had gone out because Tower #4511 had collapsed.

The rushing waters had literally bored a tunnel under the tower and an enormous gust of wind had done the rest. A shudder, a creak, a sickening swaying and clangor of steel, the angry whine and hum of electric cables stretched to their limits of endurance, then a dreadful crash. Like a nest of disturbed snakes, the snapped live cables twisted and writhed, blue sparks spitting at the rain and earth. So hot were the cable tips that in spite of the downpour they were able to set little brushfires that flared up momentarily before succumbing to the merciless beating of the rain.

Back in town, the same gust that had toppled the electrical tower had ripped from its chains the sign that said WILLIE'S BAIT: LIVE WORMS and flung it through the window of Ronnie's Fishing Post across the street. An observer with a fine sense of irony would, in the light of what was to happen in the next twenty four hours, have noted something symbolic about this. But then that observer would have had to know that Tower #4511 had been blown down and now lay in a heap of tortured metal, its cables beating the wet ground like so many high-pressure water hoses that might have twisted out of the hands of a firefighting team.

But there was no one present to observe this.

No one but the hundreds of millions of worms that inhabited every acre of ground in the vicinity of the tower, worms that, literally galvanized by the stinging electrical current that charged through their native soil, squirmed to the surface driven by desperate impulses far beyond their comprehension.

Chapter Two

Geri Sanders looked up at the shower head and frowned. Was it her imagination or had the pressure dropped?

She reached for the hot and cold knobs and turned them to their full open positions. There was a slight surge but the force of the spray was far from normal. "Damn!" she muttered. She'd been through this often enough to know what it meant: after last night's storm, a power line was down. The pump that sent water to the top of the Fly Creek water tower was therefore not operating, and before long there'd be no water at all until the power company located the downed lines and repaired them. Then she shrugged. Things could have been a lot worse, considering the fury of the storm. Some people were lucky they still had a roof over their heads, let alone electricity.,

Not knowing how much longer the pressure would stay up, she hurriedly soaped herself, running the cloth over her graceful neck, white freckled shoulders, and small, high breasts, then worked it down over her flat tummy, between her thighs, over her firm young buttocks: then finally down her long, prettily tapered legs. She raised her face to the shower head and let the needle spray course through her long auburn hair, sending the shampoo frothing over her face and down her body until it swirled around her toes and drained with a sucking noise out of the tub.

She reached for a green face towel, vigorously ran it through her hair and knotted it on the side of her head. Then she patted herself dry with a bath towel, wrapped it around her body underneath her shoulders, and rubbed the steam off the medicine cabinet mirror for a quick glance at her face.

It's not so much that Geri was vain—at least, she was no more vain than any other good looking twenty-two year old girl. No, it was just that today was a very special day, and she wanted to be absolutely sure of being as attractive as possible. She'd thought of little else for the last few weeks, and had been incapable of passing a mirror lately without scrutinizing her image for the faintest blemishes.

There were none this morning. Her skin, that translucent ivory color with which so many redheads are often blessed, was milkmaid pure, except for those darned freckles, and even they didn't look so awful because of the merest blush of a suntan she'd acquired the past two days.

She touched the mirror with a long finger, then repaired to her bedroom where she lingered before her open closet trying to select the right dress. She finally chose a violet and blue floral print that had always shown off her hazel eyes to· their best advantage. It didn't hurt her figure, either; its scoop-neck displayed the crescents of her breasts, and the short sleeves called attention to her well-turned arms. A plunging back was the final touch: whether he looked at her front, back, or profile, Mick would get an eyeful. She cast an eye at her electric clock. Damn again! It had stopped. She rummaged around the top of her night table and found her watch. Her pulse doubled as she realized that the bus carrying Mick was less than two hours away.

She tugged at the end of the towel tucked in the crease between her breasts, and it slid down her hips and fell to her feet. She held the dress up to her nose a moment, inhaling the crisp, summery, starchy aroma. Then she draped the dress over her arms and head and shimmied and wriggled until it slid over her frame and fitted itself to the contours of her shapely body. She donned the little heart locket she'd worn ever since she was a toddler, then opened her favorite perfume bottle and touched its tip to the pulse points on her wrists, throat, and breasts. She went to the window, breathed deeply of the clean, still-damp air, and spun around once with a giggle in joyous anticipation of the moment when Mick would take her in his strong arms.

Then her eyes caught sight of Roger standing in the yard abutting their property. He stood there dumbly, gaping at her with a sheepish grin plastered on his face. She felt a hot flush of embarrassment racing up her shoulders and neck and infusing her cheeks. How long had he been standing there watching her? Had he seen her naked? The thought of it made her a little queasy.

They'd grown up together, she and Roger, and were close friends in some way, closer, like brother and sister. Of course, that didn't make Roger as happy as he'd have been if he could have been her lover. But for Geri that was out of the question. Oh, sure, sometimes she'd give him a big hug and a kiss, but that was teddy bear stuff, and not to be interpreted as anything more serious. Though Roger was a good hearted soul, he was also—well . . . a little weird. Many Fly Creek girls thought him goofy in spite of his dusky good looks and athletic physique. From time to time he got a dreamy look in his eyes and no one could penetrate its significance. All Geri knew was that it frightened her a little. There was a suppressed vein of violence deep down in Roger and the thought that it might ever surface in her presence, might ever surface because of something she did or provoked, was a concern that never quite erased itself from Geri's mind.

Roger had been gathering up broken branches beneath the enormous elm tree that stood on the Sanders side of the line between the two properties. but whose branches reached over the line to the Grimes side. He'd snap the smaller ones in his hands or the larger ones over his knee and stuff them into bushel baskets, stopping occasionally to mop his brow. It was at that moment he'd straightened up to daub a trickle of perspiration from his forehead that he'd seen Geri in the window of her bedroom on the second floor of the yellow, Georgian-style house. The towel had just dropped away from her body and the glimpse of her milk-white breasts had sent a thrill of excitement through Roger's body.

He'd watched raptly she donned her dress and whirled around like a model at a fashion show, and even when she locked eyes with him and recoiled with revulsion, he'd been unable to take his eyes off her or wipe the grin off his face. For a minute they engaged in a sort of staring contest, then she broke it off, lowering her eyes and drifting away from the window. Suddenly Roger felt deeply embarrassed and foolish and returned to his work with a vengeance.

Geri trotted down the stairs on light feet and headed for the kitchen, drawn to the sound of her mother's transistor radio. The kitchen and dining room constituted an extension of the original two-story, box-shaped home, an extension that Geri's dad had built by hand a few months ago, just before he died. Geri never stepped over the threshold between the original house and the new part without thinking of her father, a strong, handsome, charming man taken before his time in a factory accident in Savannah. With him gone, responsibility for the family had naturally devolved upon Geri's mother, but lately her mother had begun to show signs of...of what? Maybe it was her change of life or something. The woman showed signs of being unable to cope, of losing grip on herself, and therefore on Geri and Geri's kid sister Alma. It saddened Geri, but it also made her uptight, because the woman had begun pushing Geri in Roger's direction in the hope of making a match, a match that would bring a strong man back into the house and relieve her of the weight of responsibility.

Naomi Sanders had flung open the kitchen window as Geri tripped into the room, and was even at this moment chatting with Roger, who'd finished picking up the debris on his side of the fence and was now working on theirs.

"That's very nice of you, Roger," Naomi Sanders was saying in her most engaging manner, "but isn't it too hot for that sort of work?"

"No problem, Mrs. Sanders," Roger shouted back. "Well, come in for a cold drink."

"Thanks. Soon as I finish this batch," the boy replied, delving into his work at double-time in anticipation of the double pleasure of refreshment and a chance to see Geri.

Mrs. Sanders shook her head as she turned away from the window. "Lord knows how Roger can work in this Godawful heat. They say it's going into the nineties today. It feels like that already." To emphasize this, she pulled the neckline of her brown dress away from her throat, to which it clung, as if to give vent to the steam that had accumulated underneath it. She smiled at Geri and held up her cheek for a daughterly kiss. Geri dutifully obliged, but it was too hot and sticky for an embrace.

Mrs. Sanders glanced one more time at Roger, then unconsciously touched her fingertips to the bun of gray hair atop her head. She was still a handsome, attractive woman and the expected presence of a man in her house stimulated her vanity.

Geri untied the knot of the towel around her own hair, which was still damp, rubbed her scalp briskly for a minute, then dropped the towel on the back of a chair and turned to wash the morning's dishes in the sink. Together they listened to the news report coming over the transistor radio. "... main roads are badly flooded, many blocked by fallen trees. All power in the area struck by the storm is out. All phone service is dead..."

Geri bit her lip as she wondered whether the bus bringing

Mick from New York would have any difficulty with flooded roads. For that matter, would she have a problem driving the car into town? The road to Fly Creek invariably flooded after a storm like last night's, catching the overflow from the marshy western end of Fly Lake. How would she pick up Mick? How would he make his way to the house?

"Have you checked the garage?" her mother's voice broke into Geri's troubled revery. "I hope nothing got flooded in the shop." Geri and her mother supplemented her father's insurance settlement by selling antiques and bric-a-brac out of their garage.

"No, I stacked everything off the floor last night," Geri said, rinsing the dishes. Washing dishes had always caused Geri's mind to wander, and she soon found it concentrating on the image of Mick, whom she'd met at an antiques fair in Atlanta. He'd obviously gotten stuck on her, but whether he felt the same way three months later—but of course he must, or he wouldn't come all this distance, would he?

Again, her mother's sharp voice intruded on her thoughts. "Oh, for heaven's sake, the fridge is off too. All the food will spoil." Geri looked over her shoulder and saw her mother standing chin in hand before the darkened box of the refrigerator, shaking her head. The woman sighed and quickly shut the door.

Her troubled eyes brightened as she seemed to notice her daughter for the first time today. "This Mick must really be something special," she said, eyes roving over Geri's frock. "This is the first time I've seen you in anything other than jeans and a sweatshirt all summer."

Geri felt her throat reddening, kissed her mother on the cheek, and picked up a dish towel. "Oh, mother, it's just so hot. I wanted to wear something light."

It was plain to see that her mother didn't buy it. "Where in New York does he live?"

"Right in the city," Geri replied, somewhat breathlessly. From all they both knew of New York, living right in the city struck them as a rather adventurous if not foolhardy thing to do.

"What kind of work does he do? Does he go to school?" Mrs. Sanders asked.,

"He went to law school. Now he's working as a clerk for a big law firm."

Mrs. Sanders turned her nose up slightly at this information. "Your father never did have any use for lawyers.".

"Maybe if he did, you would have had something set aside," Geri came back, just a tiny bit snappishly. Naomi Sanders glared at her daughter.

"Your father did the best he could. I don't remember you ever going without," she said, grabbing a dish towel of her own and polishing a plate to a gleaming shine. "Where'd you meet this Mick, anyway?"

"I told you. At the dealer's show. He was browsing around."

"And he's coming way down here just to look for antiques?" she asked with a skeptical tilt of the head.

"No," said Geri defensively. Then, "Well, partly. He gets five days off in the whole summer and he'd rather spend them down here in the country than the...mother, why are you asking?"

The question came so suddenly that Mrs. Sanders fumbled the plate in her hands and dropped it on the kitchen floor, shattering it. "Damn!" Geri stooped to pick up the shards as her mother covered her face. This was typical of how the woman had been behaving of late—jumpy and irritable. Then the mood passed with a deep breath, and she laughed. "All right, all right. I won't butt in. Just don't be too disappointed if he doesn't come. I doubt if the bus can get through. You heard what the radio said." She wrapped her hands around her arms, as if a chill wind had blown over her body despite the soaring heat of the morning. "My nerves are still jumping from that thunder. God, I never saw a storm like that. There was something....evil about it"

Geri didn't really hear her mother, for her mind was far away, had drifted magically over the miles to the bus bringing Mick, and had formed a picture of herself sitting beside him, holding his hand as the countryside whizzed past the window. "I think he'll come," she mused.

There was a low rumble in the pipes under the kitchen sink.

"Oh no!" her mother groaned.

"What now?"

They both knew what it meant Geri twisted the faucets. The water sputtered and gurgled, faltered, then surged through the pipes once again with a troubled chugging sound. Soon there'd be no water, at least not till there was electricity.

It was hard for Geri to be concerned with running water for the problem of picking Mick up over shadowed all her thoughts. Finishing up the dishes, she left the kitchen for the coolness of the living room. As she entered, she looked out the window and saw something that transformed her troubled expression into one of almost beatific rapture. "You think Roger will let me borrow his father's truck? I can cut through the woods and meet Mick on Route 41!" she said over her shoulder to her mother.

"I can't wait to meet this guy," came cynically from the living room. It was Alma, Geri's younger sister, and she punctuated this declaration with a munch of apple. "You've been yakking about him all week."

Geri peered into the dim living room where Alma sat on a couch chewing her apple and trying to read a copy of *Cosmopolitan* using the natural light filtering into the room through the gauzy curtains.

Alma Sanders bore little resemblance to her older sister. Her hair was darker, except for some reddish highlights, and was cropped in a shag cut. She was well built and fully mature for fifteen, but she was also inclined to pudginess, and it was hard to say if her weight problem was an adolescent phase or a permanent affliction. Since Alma resembled their father.

Geri suspected the girl would go through life struggling to keep her body trim, whereas for Geri with her bird-like appetite, the opposite problem prevailed.

The girl wore a coral-colored playsuit, short pants with a matching blouse that tied around her waist. On her feet she wore the faddish cork platform shoes that all the kids were wearing these days-when they weren't falling off them and breaking their ankles.

Geri didn't take too kindly to her sister's razzing about Mick, and simply glared at the girl as she entered the living room. Alma pouted, reached a long-nailed hand out for the transistor radio, and flicked on the rock station. There was an old Led Zeppelin song on, to which Alma mouthed the lyrics and plunged back into her article about the joys of white slavery.

Just then their mother came in complaining about the sink. "What else can go wrong here?" she said, though she knew neither girl was listening to her. She noticed Alma trying to read, holding the magazine close to her eyes, and snatched it out of the girl's hands. "No reading until the lights go back on, young lady. That's how you spoil your eyesight."

Alma grabbed for the magazine, but her mother pulled it out of reach. The girl groaned, then turned the music up as her mother plumped down in her overstuffed chair in the comer of the room, picked up a half-finished woolen shawl, and started to knit. Alma was tempted to remark about what a fine one her mother was to talk, trying to knit in this light, but realizing that her mother would come back with some boringly predictable answer, she dropped it and sulked.

The three of them sat that way for several minutes, Alma brooding to her rock music, Mrs. Sanders knit ting busily, and Geri preoccupied with the problem of picking Mick up from the bus. These long, slightly hostile silences had become more the rule than the exception lately, and Geri felt profound relief to know that Mick was coming to stay, even for a few days. The presence of a man around the house would do wonders for their sagging spirits, which were doubly depressed as summer entered the dogdays of August.

Of course, Roger, who hung around the Sanders' residence, could also be considered a man around the house if you stretched definitions a bit, but somehow it wasn't the same. Roger not only did not give comfort (except to Mrs. Sanders' marital expectations for Geri), he took it away. He made you vaguely uncomfortable. He stared at you just a little longer than you liked. You never knew what he was thinking. Oh, one supposed he was harmless enough, but there are degrees of harmlessness. Roger w harmless like some big stray dog whose pedigree and training you don't know. You could keep him for ten years and in the eleventh...well, who knows?

As these thoughts flitted over the screen of Geri's mind, Roger shouldered open the screen door and clumped into the house, heavy work shoes muddy and caked with dead leaves. Mrs. Sanders jumped to her feet pointing at his shoes, and he made a gesture of recognition, went out and stomped his shoes and cleaned them on the doormat, then entered again, slamming the screen door with slight irritation. Mrs. Sanders smiled and went into the kitchen to get Roger the cold drink he'd been promised—though how cold it could be with the electricity off and the refrigerator slowly defrosting, she muttered to herself, Lord only knew.

Roger stood hesitantly at the entrance to the living room, staring shyly at Geri. He was still obviously embarrassed at having been caught peeking at her as she dressed after her shower. But Geri, eager to put him at his ease, smiled engagingly and gave no acknowledgment of what had happened a little while earlier. "Hi, Roger," she chirped.

He grinned. His deep, dark, fathomless eyes, had they glowed more warmly than coldly, would have made him an irresistible catch for the girls of Fly Creek. He wore tight but well-worn and faded jeans and a white knit polo shirt out of which his muscular chest and arms fairly burst, and though he was per spired, he seemed otherwise completely unfatigued by exertions that would have caused most other young men to collapse.

Yet this big lad with the ox-like constitution seemed to turn to gelatin when Geri put her hands on his chest and said, "Can I ask you a big, big favor?"

He didn't even hesitate, didn't even raise the possibility her request might be impossible to fulfill. "Sure, Geri. You name it."

Geri was over the hump, now. The: rest was a formality. "I have to pick somebody up out on route 41. The roads are all flooded, but I bet I can make it in your truck."

Roger beamed. His impression was that this "somebody" who had to be picked up was a cousin or an aunt or a girlfriend. It didn't even cross his mind that it could be a man. "I'll drive you," he said genially.

Geri realized she was on dangerous ground. Once Roger, who fancied himself special in Geri's life, realized it was a boyfriend she was going to pick up he'd be enraged. Roger's rages were scary to behold, too, because unlike most people, who shouted, ranted, shook their fists, kicked things, stormed out of the room, cursed, or otherwise carried on, Roger simply smoldered. And it made Geri uneasy with him.

Geri fired a look at her sister that said, Keep your mouth shut. Unfortunately, though Alma was listening to the exchange, her eyes were up on the ceiling as she daydreamed and followed the tune on the radio.

Geri anxiously sought some valid reason why Roger shouldn't come with her in the truck to pick up Mick, and finally came up with one that was feeble but better than nothing. "What's the matter, afraid I can't handle it myself?"

Roger shrugged and was about to reply when Alma suddenly came back down from the clouds and shouted, "Mother, where's Mick gonna sleep? In Geri's room?".

Geri glared so hard at Alma that if looks could harm, Alma would have been riveted to the couch by a thousand arrows.

That bitch! Not only had she been following the conversation, but she'd been biding her time until she could set off the little bomb.

Roger looked like he'd just taken a shotgun blast full in the chest. Geri's face was crimson, and her eyes were full of murderous rage for her troublemaking kid sister, who coolly took another chunk of apple in her teeth and gnawed it noisily. The situation wasn't eased at all by Mrs. Sanders' reply: "He'll sleep on the cot in the extra room."

Roger shifted his weight back and forth. Geri understood full well what it meant. That ponderous mind of his was slowly but certainly picking up momentum as it grasped the significance of this Mick fellow. Geri realized she had to move fast before the boy changed his mind.

"Roger, I promise to be super careful," she said, touching his wrist tenderly and heading for the front door.

Roger wiped his mouth with the back of his hand, then nodded slowly, like a bear. "Okay, you can use it," he shouted after her as if it weren't already a *fait accompli*. "But don't upset the crate. I have a full shipment in there."

Geri gave a high sign of acknowledgment and climbed into the cab of the rusty blue van. It was actually an old Dodge panel truck that Roger's father had converted by building a customized wooden compartment to contain the crates of worms he carried into town for his bait shop or down to the other coastal towns in the areas. Painted sloppily in white on the cab door were the words: WILLIE'S BAIT, FLY CREEK, GA

The keys were in the ignition but Geri forgot to depress the clutch when she turned the switch on. The engine emitted a weird *wugga-wugga* sound and the truck leaped forward. Geri looked back at Roger and tried to make light of this dumb move, which was scarcely calculated to calm his anxieties about her driving skill.

"Geri!" her mother was shouting from the kitchen window.

Geri stuck her head out of the cab window and tilted it to pick up what her mother was saying. "See if you can pick up some ice at Kirby's. Lord knows when the fridge will go on again."

Geri saluted acknowledgment, then returned to the challenge of starting Roger's truck. With great deliberateness, tongue flicking over her lips·, Geri recited a sort of catechism of driver education. Put the gear shift in neutral. Keep the clutch depressed to the floor. Pull the throttle out a bit. Now, turn the key.

Still damp from last night's torrential storm, the engine made churning, troubled noises, *wugga-wuggawugga-wugga-cough*, before bursting into a satisfying rumble. Geri breathed a sigh of relief. She looked back at the house, where she saw three people with three very different expressions watching this display: Mother with her rather bland face, her only concern being that Geri remembered to bring home ice; Roger with a mixture of anger that he'd been duped and anxiety about the cargo in the back of the truck; and Alma with that look of amused deviltry. *That Alma!* Geri said to herself. It wasn't enough that she'd stirred up Roger. She'd have been glad to see Geri tum the truck over and let loose the whole shipment of worms upon the town. What a riot *that* would be!

Geri turned away and concentrated on the rest of the procedure. She cleared the engine's throat, a big blue cloud of smoke spewing into the air from its rusty exhaust pipe. She let it idle a moment, then pushed the throttle back in. Her foot pushed the throttle to the floor and she was about to yank the gear shift into first when she remembered the hand-brake. She twisted and released it, then put the truck into first.

She let up the clutch too slowly without stepping sufficiently on the gas. Then she gave it too much gas and lifted her foot too suddenly off the clutch. The truck lurched out of the driveway and chugged forward like a bucking horse until she at last was able to find the right combination of pressures on the clutch and gas pedals.

As she steered out of the dirt driveway and onto the Fly Creek road, which would carry her some way toward town before flood waters would necessitate a diversion over land, Geri felt her irritation with her family and Roger melting away in anticipation of her first moments with Mick.

What would he be wearing? How would he look? Would he remember her, remember the warm moments they'd shared, or would he be indifferent and require a lot of chatter and kisses and caresses.to warm him up to her again. The last time he'd been dressed rather stiffly in slacks, tie and jacket in keeping with his role as law office clerk. She hoped he wouldn't be so foolish as to dress like a dude for a country vacation. Well, if he did, she'd change that fast enough.

She'd driven about a mile and was so lost in her fantasies that she almost skidded into the two feet of water that covered Fly Creek Road at Pimm's Hollow, where Fly Lake's marshy tip had swollen and overflowed. She brought the truck to a halt, wrestled with the stick until it fell into reverse, then backed up and aimed the truck for the well-worn double track that led over the Pimm farm's grazing meadow to the woods which would bring her within a mile of Route 41—and her Mick.

The truck jounced over the rutted path, and though she tried to hold her speed down, she kept losing herself in revery, and failed to hear the creaks and groans of the crates in the back of the truck as the heavy load bottomed on useless shock absorbers.

Chapter Three

The silver National bus, with its destination, "Miami," bannered above its windshield, picked its way over the broken limbs, slippery leaves and other debris that still littered Route 41. Driver Ed Morris a round, florid-faced North Carolinian, sucked in his gut as he downshifted for the pull up Smith's Hill. He'd been over this route no fewer than two hundred times, and he knew that ,the sight that greeted him when he crested this rise would determine whether the bus made it to Miami on time, or with a delay of hours to accommodate detours, or possibly not at all if the flooding was so bad as to require him to tum back to Savannah.

The bus whined as it crept up the hill, strained at the summit, then glided down a long gentle grade and around a right-hand curve. "Aw, damn!" Morris muttered, pumping the brake. With a flatulence of released pneumatic pressure, the bus slowed and finally halted before the tremendous girth of a felled cedar. An ugly black wound, bleeding pitch, testified to the awesome power of a direct hit from a lightning bolt, its splintered, ragged trunk looking as if some giant had bent a sapling oxer his knee. Morris cursed again, sighed, put the bus in neutral, and tipped his hat back on his head. "This is as far as we can go, folks. I'll turn around and backtrack to Williamstown. That's the best I can do."

A collective groan went up from the dozen or so passengers who remained on the bus on this last leg of the New York-Miami run. It had been a long, hard ride, as their disheveled clothes and worn expressions mutely declared, and now this—this was the final blow.

They gazed in despair at the downed tree and the expanse of muddy water on the other side of it. The rest of Route 41 picked up like a severed ribbon about five hundred yards on the other side of this temporary artificial lake, beckoning ironically like a seductress tempting them to their doom. But they knew that even if that downed tree were somehow removed, the water hazard could not be braved: it would be almost five feet deep at its low point, too deep to accommodate the bus.

In the back of the bus, a young man lay curled in fetal position across two of the hot corduroy-covered seats. He'd been sleeping, or at least trying to sleep, and the driver's announcement had somehow filtered through the fog and penetrated his brain. He opened one eye and peered, mole-like, over his arm and down the aisle. The bus was on a slight angle downward and he could see an expanse of brackish water before it. He'd heard the driver mention Williamstown, and now remembered being told that Williamstown would be the last stop before Fly Creek.

All at once he popped to an upright position, shouting, "Wait! I'll get out here."

The driver opened the door and Mick Gordon hurriedly hauled his belongings from the luggage rack and the space under his seat. This was no mean feat, as he seemed to have collected the combined inventories of a sporting goods store, army-navy store, and a camping equipment shop. After fumbling with an enormous backpack, a set of fins, snorkel and mask, a tennis racket, and a fishing pole, he began edging down the aisle, apologizing profusely as he bumped a lady's head with his backpack, impaled a man with his tennis racket, and managed to stick the tip of his fishing rod into the ear of a grandmother who made her displeasure known in no uncertain terms.

"Sorry," Mick breathed, trying to smile bravely.

"Excuse me. Sorry. Sorry."

At last he arrived at the front of the bus, where the driver sat mopping the back of his neck with a hand kerchief. The man looked at Mick for a long moment, shaking his head at the sight of this slightly built, pale-skinned fellow decked out in enough paraphernalia to equip a summer camp.

Mick sensed he must look slightly ridiculous, but what the hell could a man do? If the bus had made it into town the way it was supposed to, this wouldn't have happened.

"Do you have any maps of the area, sir?" he asked respectfully.

The driver glared at him, wondering if this wise ass from New York City was putting him on. "Where you goin'?"

"Fly Creek?"

The driver gestured with his chin and hand: straight ahead.

"Can you give me some directions?" Mick pressed. His legal training had come in handy: if the witness doesn't give you a specific enough answer, have another go at him till he does.

But the driver ducked out of it. "Straight ahead. But you'll need a boat." Then he studied the load of gear on Mick's back. "I'm sure you got one back there someplace," he added, chuckling.

Mick had to admit the man had gotten off a good one at his expense, but before the door could close he asked, "By the way, you wouldn't know where a person could take a leak around here?"

The driver's face dropped, and his reply was the slam of the bus door, leaving Mick on his own. After an intricate maneuver, the driver managed to get the bus's direction reversed, and the throaty music of its engine soon faded into the stillness of midmorning, and Mick was alone on the edge of a swampy woods that extended God only knew how far. Well, he reflected, here's an opportunity to test out my camping equipment and skills. The problem was, the equipment was brand new and the skills practically unused, the product of a lot of book-learning and almost no experience.

He sighed, listening to the silence, then plunged in. Straight ahead, the driver said. Okay, goddammit, Mick was going to go straight ahead, and Heaven help the tree, bog, or predatory animal that got in his way.

But first—that leak.

Mosquitoes swarmed around him as he relieved himself against the trunk of an oak tree, and he hastily zippered his fly against the onslaught of one particularly horny mosquito. You can have the back of my neck, he told it under his breath, but leave *that* part of me alone.

As he was picking up his gear there was a splintering crack over his head and he had to dance out of the way to avoid a big dead branch that had almost diabolically waited until Mick was under it before giving up the ghost.

Mick sighed, then, hands shaking, he reached into his pocket and produced a cigarette and a disposable butane lighter. The impact of the smoke on his lungs relaxed him considerably as he contemplated his journey. Though the woods were dense, even the small amount of sun penetrating to the floor of the forest was blazing hot, and the damp heat of the moldering leaves beneath his feet made the air intolerably sticky. He doffed his blue windbreaker, reached into his pack and hauled out a blue tee-shirt, still wrapped in the plastic bag it had come in at The Gap. The Gap! New York City seemed to be on another planet, he reflected as he yanked the tag off the tee-shirt. What the hell am I doing here, anyway, when I could be playing soft ball in Central Park?

He'd met Geri Sanders at this antiques fair—he was passionately interested in crystal, and Geri just happened to have a handsome piece of Lalique. nestled among the routine stuff at her stand. He'd asked her how much she wanted for it, and when she told him, he'd said, "That's not enough. I'll give you twice that," and so stunned the svelte hazel-eyed redhead that she'd dropped the crystal decanter. Mick. horrified, stuck his foot out instinctively to prevent it from shattering. He'd succeeded, at the cost of a bruised instep. Naturally, Geri had to nurse it, and that was the start of their romance.

But that had been months ago, and though they'd written each other and talked several times on the phone, he seriously wondered if she really remembered him, let alone cared for him as much as she had then. Indeed, to be perfectly honest about it, he wasn't sure any more how strong his own feelings were. This would be a good opportunity to pit against each other those two warring proverbs, Absence Makes the Heart Grow Fonder *vs.* Out of Sight, Out of Mind, to see which was the more truthful. He knew which one he was rooting for, of course. Hell, for all the trouble he was going to, doing this Livingstone-Stanley expedition through the jungles of darkest Georgia, Geri's heart had damn well better have grown fonder, he thought bitterly, as he slapped himself nearly senseless against a swarm of hungry mosquitoes. He reached into his pack and pulled out a can of 10-49 insect repellent. He sprayed himself liberally on the neck and arms, then put some on his hand and smeared it on his face. Repel lent was the right word for it. There wasn't an insect alive that would dare come within a yard of him, and as for snakes and other nasty creatures, he doubted if they'd hazard an attack on the bizarre creature with a life-support system on his back, and what appeared to be several dangerous weapons clutched in his hands. And thus he trudged, for what seemed an hour but was probably considerably less. Ugly blue sweat-stains marred the chest, back, and underarms of his new tee-shirt, his shoulders ached from the unaccustomed load of a backpack and the chafe of the straps on the thin cotton of his shirt. and the muscles of his thighs and calves began to cramp and throb.

In spite of it all. he was feeling rather proud of himself. After all, the purpose of this vacation was to get back to nature, and here he was confronting nature eyeball-to-eyeball. If it didn't kill him, it would probably be good for him.

He had no sooner enunciated this thought than he found himself exactly eyeball-to-eyeball with a patch of flooded ground around the roots of a cypress tree. He looked to both sides and the ground looked no drier, and besides, he was reluctant to. veer from the straight-arrow path he'd determined to follow. Though the Okefenokee Swamp was still many hundreds of miles to the south, this territory was sufficiently rural for a man to get himself permanently lost. So there was nothing for it but to plunge straight through the wet spot.

And plunge he did: at least four feet worth. The wet patch turned out to be the surface of a boggy hole at least that deep, and the intrepid woodsman plummeted up to his armpits into a morass of vile-smelling muck. For a moment his heart sank— literally—as his boot-toes found no purchase whatsoever, and he struggled to get the straps of his pack down over his shoulders before it pulled him under. Then he located a solid root, which at least bought him a moment to think.

Okay, the first thing I do is chuck my tennis racket and fishing pole on the dry ground on the other side of this hole, he determined. Then, off comes the pack and it goes beside my sporting goods. Then I look for something solid my fingers can get a hold on, and haul my behind out of here.

Relieving himself of these items, he reached for what he thought was an exposed cypress root, but it turned out to be a dead branch lying on the forest floor, and he fell back into the fen, submerging this time up to his chin.

He heard a titter.

Had he not recognized the graceful tinkle of the titter's voice. he might have thought it was a goblin come to divert herself at his expense. He looked up and there she was, the girl he'd come by land and mud to see. For an instant he relaxed in his boggy prison, drinking in the sight of her slim figure snugly clothed in a purple frock, her long auburn hair glinting in a fugitive ray of sunlight, her bright eyes and clear complexion. He now knew the meaning of the cliche, a sight for sore eyes.

Then he realized what he must look like. It was not precisely what he'd had in mind for a grand entrance.

Luckily for him, Geri had a sense of humor, and though he felt like a stupid ass, Geri didn't appear to be thinking any less of him for his predicament. Nevertheless, it would be a bad idea to test how long she would find it amusing; another minute of floundering and she might begin to think he was a stupid ass too. That would never do. Testing another root and finding it firmly attached to its tree, he hauled himself out of there with a mighty effort.

Geri gazed, mouth parted in a smile and eyes twinkling with good humor, as the muddy water drained in a widening circle around his feet. In what had to be the profoundest understatement since "Dr. Livingstone, I presume," Mick said, "Hey, Geri. How you been?"

Her engaging smile told him everything.

Chapter Four

"I'll get you some dry clothes when we get to my house," she said as they made their way toward the truck. Glancing at Mick's gear, she added, "Wow. It looks like you're ready for action."

Mick shrugged, feeling slightly dumb and embarrassed. "I just picked up a few things."

Mick tilted his head at the wording on the side of the truck. "Where'd you get this?"

"You like?" Geri laughed. "It's the latest model."

They climbed into the truck and looked at each other a moment, and for that moment the mud-caked Mick disappeared into the good-looking, good-humored young man she'd met a few months ago. She raised her lips for a kiss, but in Mick's own mind, the good-looking, good-humored young man was still a mud-caked fool, and he merely touched his lips to her cheek to avoid smudging her. There would be plenty of time for deeper kisses.

Geri wrinkled her nose and rolled her window down. Mick got the hint and rolled his own down, moving as close to the door on his own side as he could.

"What kind of bait does Willie sell?" he asked.

"Worms."

Mick turned around and peered through the rear window of the truck's cab. "Any back there?"

"Crates of them," Geri replied.

"Live?"

"Live and wiggly," Geri said, with slightly devilish gusto. She was fairly certain how a city boy would react to the notion of crates and crates of live and wiggly worms.

She was right. "Yucchh," he said.

"It's my neighbor's truck," Geri explained. "He runs a worm farm."

"Do they eat worms around here?" he asked, keeping a straight face.

Geri sighed exasperatedly, not realizing he was putting her on. "No, dummy. They raise them for bait. He has a store in town."

She started the engine, turned the truck around, and headed for home. "Tell me about your trip," she said. "Did you have any trouble in the storm?"

"I guess we missed it," Mick said. "We had clear sailing until we got near Fly Creek. Then the driver had to turn around. Hey, how'd *you* get here?"

"I took a back way through the woods," Geri explained. "A bus could never make it through there."

They jounced over the unpaved road, then onto a tarred one scarcely any smoother. For a moment they did not speak, reveling in the happiness of being reunited. Then Mick spoke, sounding a serious note.

"Hey, Geri, I'm really sorry to hear about your father. Must have been pretty rough." Geri opened her mouth to say something, but what could she say? The man had suffered more, she felt irrationally, than a human should be made to suffer. The mere mention of it tied her tongue. "You have any brothers and sisters? You never mentioned in your letters," Mick added.

"One sister and my mother."

"How're they taking it?"

"Alma's okay," Geri said uncertainly. "It's really hard to tell with her. But Mom's taking it very hard. She's been a nervous wreck."

"What are you doing for money?" Mick asked. He was only trying to be helpful, but then, realizing how indiscreet it might have sounded to her, added, "Uh, sorry..."

Geri held up a hand. "It's okay. I'm running the business. Before Dad had the accident I was doing a lot of the refinishing and selling Oh, by the way, I'm going to take you to the greatest antique shop today."

Mick beamed. There was nothing he'd like so much—unless it was to get into some clean, dry clothes.

Geri slowed the truck down and wrenched the wheel right, shifting down into second gear. The truck whined and buckled over a muddy road that cut through a thin wood. A few branches beat at the truck and squeaked over the metal fenders and doors. She hit one pothole a little too fast and the cargo of crates thundered in the back of the truck. Mick made a face. The thought of all those worms escaping from their confinement made him shiver with disgust.

Geri took the rest of the road more carefully, and after a minute or two more they were back on a paved road. And a moment later, civilization! Well, not really civilization, Mick thought, rebuking himself for his insufferable New York City snobbery, but at least Fly Creek was the most civilization he'd seen since getting off the bus.

Fly Creek was an anthill of activity as its residents and shop-keepers cleaned up after the storm. The streets still glistened with water, leaves, twigs, and branches still littered lawns, streets, and sidewalks. Here and there could be seen scattered shingles, which Mick traced to a patch of bare roof on a saltbox house just off the main street. On the main street, itself, several stores sported broken windows. damaged facades, downed electrical wires. The hot sun beating down out of a cloudless sky sent steam rippling into the air, giving the town a misty aura. Above, a few squeaking seagulls reminded Mick that this was a coastal town.

Geri pulled up in front of a gas station beside which was an ice machine. "I promised my mother I'd get some ice. All our electricity is out."

"Yeah?"'

"And the phones."

"Must have been a dilly of a storm," Mick murmured respectfully.

Geri shook her head, still a little shocked by the intensity of the experience. "Mick, it was incredible. Like a war. Everything was lit up. And the wind, and the thunder. Oh, wow!"

"Sorry I missed it," Mick said, not quite sincerely. "I like a good thunderstorm once in a while." He slid a little closer to Geri. "Makes you feel helpless, which is kind of nice once in a while, don't you think?"

An electric charge seemed to spark between their eyes as Geri read his meaning clearly. She answered him mutely with a loving look, then pulled up the handle of her door. "I'll only be a minute," she murmured, touching the back of his hand before departing.

Mick sat still in the cab of the truck, taking in the town of Fly Creek. It was an ordinary enough town, which for a city dude was extraordinary enough since he rarely got to see a building smaller than six stories high, rarely got to see foliage that did not belong to an artificially constructed city park, rarely got to see the curving contours of hills, valleys, winding roads. In the city it was all straight lines, horizontals and verticals, sharply delineated east, west, north, south, up, down. The commonness of the old barber shop, the prim little hotel, the luncheonette, the package store, took on for Mick almost as much charm as he'd have experienced sitting in the plaza of some European town.

The only things that spoiled it for him were the crates full of worms on the other side of the steel and glass partition behind him. It was odd how the thought that—gosh, how many worms would fit back there anyway?— well anyway, all those worms sitting a few inches from your back could taint an otherwise delightful experience.

Then came the bump.

It must have been his imagination, conjuring up the notion of a bunch of angry worms sore at him for thinking bad thoughts about them. Yes, Mick decided a thrill of fear running down the flesh of his back, it was definitely his imagination. He was so certain he'd imagined that bump in the back of the truck that he decided to get the hell out of there. He climbed out of the truck and strode in the direction of Millie's Luncheonette, trying not too successfully, to control the pace of his footsteps so as not to give any indication he wanted to put as much distance as possible between himself and that truckful of worms.

God, worms! Mick said to himself, ambling past the Fishing Post where two men were cleaning up its broken plate glass window. What kind of creeperoos would farm *worms*?

Mick walked around a man carrying a piece of plywood to the Fishing Post window to cover the exposure until plate glass could be ordered. Then he stepped over the feet of some young campers stranded in town, chugging Cokes in front ·of a general store. People stopped to stare at him, and he realized that despite his muddy clothes his pale skin, well-groomed sandy hair, and eyeglasses marked him as a city tourist.

He stepped into Millie's and immediately had second thoughts about the charm of small towns. It was dreary and hot. The electricity had been knocked out by the storm, and the only light coming in filtered through an unwashed front window. Near the screen door as he walked in were racks of comic books, girlie magazines, men's adventure magazines, and some well-fingered paperback novels. Along one wall was a counter containing all sorts of things ranging from candies to practical jokes that looked distinctly corny and unfunny. Two boys stood before it, making their selection.

There were some farmhand types sitting in booths or at the greasy counter, nursing their morning coffee or sipping Dr. Pepper through straws. A stiff-spined blond man wearing a khaki uniform also sat at the counter, drinking coffee morosely and watching the blowsy redhead behind the counter over the top of his cup. As Mick straddled a stool at the counter, this man swiveled his head and studied Mick professionally, and a slight curl of the man's clean-shaven lip suggested he didn't particularly like what he saw. Mick glanced over, gave a friendly smile as he noted the Sheriff's badge on the man's shirt, but, getting no friendly smile in return, shrugged and turned away.

Mick listened to the old-timers talking about the storm in their lilting drawls. Millie, refilling the cup of one grizzled character in overalls and red flannel work shirt, asked about a family named Cutter who always seemed to be the first victims of local flooding due to their location at the end of Fly Lake.

"They took the brunt of it all right," the farmer said. "I hear old Wally had to get out with a row boat. They'll be pumping till Christmas."

Millie paused to take some change from the two little boys who'd decided to take some long red wormlike licorice whips and a practical joke called Doggie Poo that they thought might be cute to leave lying on somebody's carpet. Cute.

"I hear a whole electrical tower went down," Millie commented, returning with a damp rag to the counter. She swiped at it a few times, but as far as Mick could see she merely redistributed the thin veneer of grease that coated the Formica.

"Luckily it didn't start a fire," the sheriff observed. "All that juice pouring into the ground. Over a million amps."

"When are they to get the lines up?" Millie asked with an edge in her voice. "Before I go out of business, I hope."

"They're sending men up from Scranton. They promised to

have it straightened out by tomorrow morning," the sheriff said confidently.

"Yeah," sneered Millie. "And in the meantime, all that electricity going into the ground, and guess who's paying for it." She gave a what-are-you-gonna-do shrug and looked around for something to do or someone to serve. That's when she remembered Mick, who'd become so absorbed in the conversation, he'd forgotten to ask for anything. "Yeah, honey, what'll it be?" Millie asked.

Without hesitating, Mick said, "I'll have a large egg cream and a glass of water, please."

Every head in the luncheonette turned and focused on the pale-skinned, four-eyed intellectual kid who'd just made this bizarre request. Millie glowered, her eyebrows knitting together beneath furrowed brows. "I got the water. But what was that? An...aik-cream?"

"Egg cream," Mick pronounced with exaggerated inflections, and it was only then that he realized that egg creams were not universally known the way, say, Coca-Cola was. He could have kicked himself for personifying the typical New Yorker who believes the whole world thinks the same way he does. Now he had to explain what an egg cream was, which probably would make things worse, for, when you broke it down into its components, it sounded a little nauseating. "Just chocolate syrup, a little milk, and some seltzer water," he said, smiling feebly.

Millie tilted her head and roved the ceiling with her eyes, seeking in the dim recesses of her mind some way of associating egg creams with something in her experience. Ah, a light went on in her skull. "A chocolate soda."

"That's it," Mick beamed, looking as pleased as if he'd just managed to communicate with a native of some Pacific island. "With a little shot of milk to give it a head."

Shrugging her shoulders, and exchanging glances with the amused customers, she began assembling the components for this challenging concoction. What normally took a street corner soda jerk fifteen seconds in New York City, took Millie some two minutes. After all, Mick had mentioned three ingredients, but he hadn't described their proportions.

"Yep," said another old-timer. "Why, that was the worst storm I can remember around here since I was a tot. 'Course, there was the one in...uh, thirty-seven. But that was snow."

Millie put the finishing touch on the egg cream, and served up, with a proud smile, a glass of what appeared to be brown-colored foam to the youth at the counter. "How's that, dear?"

Mick's disappointment was inexpressible, but he smiled bravely and said, "Fine." He dropped a straw into it, sucked, but getting nothing but air for his troubles, put the straw down and sipped from the glass directly. A foam mustache was his reward.

" 'Course," another old man was saying, "there was the storm we had about three years ago. All that thunder and lightning scared them tourists right out of their shorts. Never seen anybody row that fast trying to get off that bay, dropping their fishing rods and what have you." The old man found this notion particularly humorous and burst into a hissing laugh, and was joined by the others. Mick morosely nursed his drink, wondering how anyone could call country humor funny.

Mick raised the glass to his lips and was about to tilt it upright in the hopes of extracting some liquid from the bubbles when he noticed in the bottom of the glass an ingredient that had never, to his knowledge, appeared in any egg cream created in the greater New York area.

It was solid, but so coated with liquid and foam that he couldn't distinguish it absolutely. As he reached into the glass with a long index finger, his mind flashed associations with the practical jokes and red licorice whips sold at the candy counter. For the thing in his glass did look like a licorice whip, and was probably a practical joke played on the dude from New York City. Ha ha, very funny.

It was not so funny when the licorice whip squirmed

violently between Mick's fingers and tried to bite him with two hideous, fanglike little teeth. He dropped the thing, uttering an involuntary cry, and jumped off the stool.

Millie, the sheriff, and everyone else in the luncheonette spun their heads as one.

Eyes wide, Mick pointed at the slimy thing flip flopping on the counter in a pool of chocolate milk. "There's a worm in my egg cream, lady!" he cried.

Millie stepped closer to the counter and inspected the writhing creature, then reached down, produced a washcloth, covered the worm with it and bunched up the cloth. She squeezed hard and disposed of the worm, washcloth and all, in the garbage can. Then she returned to the counter, glaring angrily at Mick.

"If you didn't like the drink, all you had to do was say so," she hissed, brushing a lock of orange hair out of her eye. "I have enough troubles today without comedians."

"What!" Mick burst out. The men at the counter leaned closer to take in the exchange, which would undoubtedly provide them with anecdotal material for years to come. "I found it in the glass," Mick protested. "I didn't *put* it there."

As if defending her maidenly virtue itself, Millie said, "Those glasses are hand-cleaned. I keep this place spotless. Never had that happen before."

"Well," Mick protested righteously, "it happened now and it's not a good way to win over new customers, if you want to be objective about it."

Suddenly Mick was aware of a dark shadow eclipsing the light coming in from the window. He looked up at the imposing figure of the sheriff, who'd gotten off his stool and was peering down at him menacingly.

"Now, why'd you go and do a juvenile thing like that, fella?" His voice was pebbly. His blue eyes were ice-cold and all business. Mick opened his mouth to reply, but decided that in the mood the sheriff was in, just about any answer would be misinterpreted. So Mick said nothing.

"Where you from, fella?"

"The city, most likely," Millie chimed in.

Mick knew a bad situation when he saw one. He rose, reaching into his pocket for some change.

"I don't want your money," Millie growled. "Just be on your way."'

The sheriff clapped an iron-like hand on Mick's shoulder, thrusting him back down on his stool. "Don't you think an apology is in order, fella?"

Bad situation or not, that was too much. "Apologize for what? Finding a worm in my egg cream?"

The sheriff glared at him with those disconcertingly icy eyes. "What business do you have in Fly Creek?"

"No business," Mick said sarcastically, "just pleasure." He rose from his stool again and walked out, feeling an itch in his spine where, irrationally, he expected a slug from the sheriff's revolver to enter momentarily.

Chapter Five

As Mick approached the truck, he saw Geri struggling with an enormous block of ice that looked like it weighed a ton. He took it off her hands and climbed into the passenger seat. "You'll have to hold it," she said, looking around and realizing there was no room for it anywhere else but Mick's lap. "I guess you can't get any wetter than you are."

That was not strictly true. The block of ice between his legs made him considerably wetter than he had been, to say nothing of making him. cooler than he wanted to be, however hot the day. As Geri started the engine, Mick looked ruefully back at Millie's Luncheonette.

"Why is everybody around here so unfriendly?"

Ignorant of the incident in the luncheonette, Geri shrugged and spoke benignly about small town ways. "Oh, they're really very nice people. But they're suspicious of strangers. The tourists pollute the lake and bay."

"Well," Mick said indignantly, "I'm not a tourist. I'm a..." The ice had at least cooled off his anger, and he managed a small joke. "I'm a Libra."

The trip back was uneventful, if you can call sitting soaking wet with a block of ice between your legs and a truckful of worms at your back uneventful. From time to time Geri took her eyes off the road to glance affectionately at her boyfriend. Her loving looks didn't make Mick any drier, but at least they made his cold wetness a little easier to bear.

After a ten minute drive, the truck pulled into the dirt driveway shared by the Sanders and the Grimes. Mick hoped that the ramshackle house on the left wasn't Geri's, and his hope was fulfilled. They pulled into the Grimes' driveway. Geri shut off the engine and left the key in the ignition. They got out and crossed to the pretty, well-kept yellow house with the four white pillars skirting a verandah and a huge elm tree casting a cooling shadow over what appeared to be a recent addition.

The beat of rock music assaulted their ears as they entered the dim hallway and looked into the living room where Alma sat, slightly out of breath as if (Mick guessed) she'd been peeping out of the windows to catch sight of Geri's boyfriend and then rushed back to her seat to assume a casual pose as he entered. Mrs. Sanders sat in a comfortable armchair busying herself with knitting.

"Mother," Geri beamed, "this is Mick." She waved her hand at Mick as if he were some prize sculpture, and her love-filled eyes were blinded to the fact that he was muddy, dirty, and carried a heavy block of ice. "Mick, my sister Alma."

Mick could hardly reach out and shake hands, but he did manage to wiggle his fingers from under the ice block. He realized it felt a little lighter, and when he looked down it appeared to have lost about twenty percent of its bulk thanks to melting. And guess where that twenty percent had gone? Into his pants, was where.

"Mick went for an unscheduled swim. He's soaked through."

Mrs. Sanders rose from her chair and clucked solicitously. "Give him some of daddy's old clothes. They're upstairs in storage. They'll be a little big, though. Your father was built much bigger up here," she said, gesturing at Mick's chest and shoulders. The three women seemed totally oblivious to Mick's predicament. Not even the goosepimples on his arms suggested that somebody ought to take the ice off his hands. Finally Geri noticed the puddle forming on the floor around his feet. "Oops," she said. "Let's get that in the kitchen."

She led him into the kitchen and opened the refrigerator door. Mick pushed the ice block into the darkened refrigerator, half smiling at the fact that the block was now almost half the size it had been when Geri shoved it into his lap in town.

Finally rid of his load, Mick began to relish the idea of a shower and clean clothes. Alas, as little as it was to ask, he was destined not to realize this dream quite yet.

"Oh Mick, wait until you see Mr. Beardsly's store. He's got the greatest old stuff," Geri said breathlessly. "You'll go crazy. And he's very reasonable. I mean, you can bargain with him."

She looked up at the clock on the wall over the sink. Mick did too, but the clock made no sense.

"I forgot," Geri said. "The clock stopped. What time do you have?"

Mick checked his watch. "About eleven-twenty."

Geri frowned. "I arranged to meet Mr. Beardsly at his store at eleven-thirty. He's opening it just for us. We'll have to hurry." In utter disregard of Mick's comfort, she turned to her mother. "Mother, Mick and I are taking the car to Beardsly's."

She took Mick by the hand and tugged. Mick followed her complacently.

"What about the dry clothes?" Mrs. Sanders asked, looking with compassion at Mick.

"It'll just have to wait till we get back," Mick sighed as Geri yanked him out the door.

She led him to a blue Ford station wagon, and as they climbed in Mick noticed two men on the Grimes side of the property arguing. One was gray-haired and stooped, with a yellow plaid shirt and overalls, and he was chewing out a young man in his early twenties, a good-looking fellow in blue jeans, a knit white shirt, and an abundance of black hair. The latter was obviously employed by the farmer, but there was something in their features that suggested kinship.

Meanwhile. Geri was starting the car and talking a mile a minute. "He has real strange old stuff," Mick heard her saying while he concentrated his attention on the argument across the way. "When somebody dies around here, he moves in like a vulture. He gets the greatest deals; roll-top desks, Tiffany lamps, you name it." She backed out of the driveway and spun the steering wheel.

"I wonder what's happening over there?" Mick mused.

"Oh, they're always fighting," Geri explained. "That's Willie Grimes and his son Roger. They own the worm farm. Willie's such a grump. He's always hounding Roger to do things."

But accustomed as she was to the Grimes quarrels, even Geri had to admit that this one seemed pretty intense. As she pulled past the parked worm truck, she noticed Roger gesturing to her, waving his arms for her to stop. She, jammed on the brakes, almost striking the boy as he stepped in front of the car. She rolled down her window and Roger thrust his face through, his jaw jutting with indignation. She noted his eyes were damp as if he'd been fighting to hold back tears. "Geri, you know I'm responsible for this truck. I only lent it to you because you promised—"

Geri's mouth dropped "What's wrong?"

Roger walked to the truck and flung open the back doors. Willie stood beside them, his cheeks huffing with anger. "The crates are empty," Roger declared, waving his arms at the vast empty darkness in the back of the truck.

Geri could only gape. "But I never *left* the truck," she protested. Then she added, "Except to get ice." She looked at Mick questioningly.

"It's strange to *me*," he hastened to put in. "I didn't let them out."

Roger returned to the car and peered at his rival. "Then who did?"

"...hundred thousand," Roger's father was fuming. "that's three hundred dollars' worth, boy."

"Look, Roger," Geri reasoned, trying to take the fuse out of this explosive situation, "maybe the door was loose and you forgot to close the crates."

"Damn right he forgot," Roger's father hollered. "His mind's always on other things." It was plain from his disapproving stare that he was referring to Geri. Then he returned his wrathful gaze to Roger. "Try to run a business. There'll be no more lending of my truck, you understand? It's going to take me the good part of a week to replace them worms and you'll be diggin' deep." He slammed Roger in the shoulder blades with the heel of his hand. It made a resounding thump, but injured the strong lad's pride worse than it did his body. Roger drew himself up, as if con templating retaliation, then skulked away.

Geri got out of the station wagon, ran past Mr. Grimes with a scornful glance, and caught up to Roger. With a hand on his arm she said, "Roger, I'm really sorry. Is there anything I can do?" She could feel his bitterness through her fingertips. He shook his head. She squeezed his arm and said, "Well, we'll see you later, then, okay?"

"Poor guy," Mick said as they pulled away from the unhappy scene. "His father was right. The way Roger looks at you I'm surprised he hasn't driven the truck into a wall yet."

Geri supposed she ought to be flattered, but the thought simply depressed her. "Sometimes he frightens me."

Geri reflected as she turned right onto a paved road. "Maybe we can help replace them somehow," she said.

For a moment Mick didn't understand what she was referring to. Then, startled, he blurted out. "A hundred thousand worms?"

Geri laughed. "What's the matter, afraid of worms?"

Mick puffed out his chest, waved his hand derisively, and

sneered, "Me? Afraid of worms?" After giving the matter a moment's consideration, he answered his own question. "Yeah."

"There's nothing to be afraid of," said Geri. "As long as you hold them by the tail."

"Why's that?"

"They bite," she declared matter-of-factly.

Mick gulped. He'd never heard of worms that bite. Actually, aside from worms he'd bought at bait shops whenever he went fishing—and *they'd* never bitten—he'd had nothing to do with worms, which was, he concluded, as it should be. He'd have nothing to do with worms and would be more than content if the worms made it mutual.

"The worms around here are all *glycera*—'blood worms'—from the ocean."

"How do you know which end is the tail?"

"The one," Geri explained with a straight face, "opposite the end that bites you."

After a few minutes Geri slowed down and swerved onto a muddy dirt and gravel driveway that led to an old, decrepit brick and wood house, dark green paint flaking off in unwholesome patches. Several warped white wooden pillars barely supported a verandah that looked as if it was about to collapse. The house was surrounded by a yard filled with rusting junk ranging from refrigerators to a set of children's swings.

They got out of the car, surveying the house through a haze that had steamed up beneath the blazing sun. The house looked eery and deserted. and the crunch of their footsteps on gravel as they approached amplified their irrational sense of anxiety created by the ghostly mist that swirled around the brick chimneys.

"One favor," Geri whispered, touching Mick's arm affectionately as they approached the side door. "Even if you don't see anything you like, please buy something?"

"Gotcha," said Mick.

Geri knocked on the door and they waited. And waited. And waited.

"Maybe he had second thoughts about opening just for us and went fishing or something," Mick said.

Geri shook her head. That didn't sound like Mr. Beardsly. "No, he promised," she said, walking over to a side window and peeking inside. She saw the cluttered parlor she'd been in many times, but no sign of life. "Mr. Beardsly?" she called. "Hello?"

Mick went to another window and peered through glass that looked as if it had never been washed. He tapped on it and waited.

Geri's look of curiosity became one of concern, and she circled around to the back of the house calling Mr. Beardsly's name. Frustrated, she stood with her hands on hips wondering what to do next.

And that's when she heard the crack. It sounded like a branch breaking, followed by a patter, as of footsteps. She padded over the weedy turf to investigate.

And she found something.

Something that froze her heart and brought screams of horror to her throat.

Chapter Six

Mick seemed to have traversed the distance from the side of the house to the side of Geri in a fraction of a moment. He found her standing before a ditch at the end of the backyard lawn, near the edge of the woods. Her hands were clutched to her cheeks, her face was drained of blood, and her eyes bulged. She was still as a statue and didn't appear to be breathing as she gazed down at something lying at her feet.

"What happened?" Mick asked, heart tripping. He followed Geri's line of vision to her feet. "Whoa!" he yelped, hopping back instinctively.

It was a skeleton.

A human skeleton, half buried in the mud.

In a few seconds, overcoming his revulsion, Mick kneeled to inspect it more closely. He noted that the soil in which it lay was freshly turned, as if someone had taken a spade to it.

The next thing he observed was that there was not a shred of clothing on or around the skeleton. And the skeleton itself seemed to be of recent vintage, indeed it glistened as if someone —or something—had polished it with an oil cloth. Mick had seen old skeletons when he visited his friends in medical school. Those had been yellow and brittle, not ivory white like this one.

"Who do you suppose it is?" he gasped.

Geri finally found her voice. "It could be a hunter. Every deer season you hear about somebody who disappeared in the woods. My father actually saw one of them shoot another hunter by mistake."

They stared at it for another minute, transfixed by its mute mystery. Then Mick straightened up, wiping off his hands. "I think one of us should go get the Sheriff." They looked at each other, and it was plain that the task of babysitting for this skeleton was not going to be one of life's profounder pleasures. "I'll stay here, okay?" Mick said chivalrously.

"Okay," Geri quickly agreed.

As she started the car, Mick looked again at the skeleton, then at the dark, foreboding woods aswirl with mist. Suddenly his chivalry encountered an entirely opposite virtue, discretion, which the proverb describes as the better part of valor. "Uh, Geri?" he shouted, breaking into a trot. "I'd better go with you."

Geri smiled. Cowardice under these circumstances was nothing to be ashamed of.

In the car, Mick attempted to divert attention from the sickening thing they'd just viewed. "After we get the Sheriff, how about a little tennis?"

"Sure," said Geri. "I wouldn't be any good. though. I never really played before."

As soon as she'd said it she gulped, realizing her goof.

Mick picked up on it at once, eyeing her critically. "You wrote in your letters that you were another Chris Evert."

"Well," the embarrassed girl said. trying to make light of it, "I did play in gym class. The teacher said I had great potential." She paused a moment, then tried a surefire way of getting out of being caught in a fib. "You can teach me."

"No I can't," Mick said, flushing with his own embarrassment. In response to Geri's shocked look, he admitted, "My racket still has the price tag on it. I've never played either."

They laughed.

"Then it's settled." Geri announced. "We'll go fishing."

To get to the sheriff's office they had to go back into town. The road took them past Geri's house, and she hit the brakes as they zoomed by. "That's funny," she murmured, putting the station wagon into reverse. "Sheriff Reston is at my house."

"Convenient," Mick said. His stomach, still a little fluttery from that skeleton, now acted up at the thought of again seeing the man who'd given him such a hard time at the luncheonette earlier this morning.

Reston was talking to Geri's mother in front of the garage, whose doors were opened to reveal a clutter of old furniture in various stages of repair, along with knick-knacks, antiques, old books and musty magazines, pictures, lamps, and just plain junk.

The sheriff was examining a tray of costume jewelry when he saw Geri and Mick ambling up purposefully. He seemed considerably less than thrilled to see Mick again.

"Here she is," Mrs. Sanders said to him. To Geri, she said, "Sheriff Reston wants to pick up a little something for Mrs. Reston."

Geri waved away formalities. "Mr. Reston, we were...This is my friend Mick."

"We've met," the sheriff said, looking contemptuously at the young man and declining to offer his hand.

"We were just heading into town to get you. We found a skeleton in back of Beardsly's Antiques."

The sheriff scarcely looked up from the jewelry tray. "Did you show it to Beardsly?" he asked with a dry smile. "He'd give you top dollar for it."

Mick didn't find it funny. "He wasn't around. I think you should look at it."

The sheriff eyed Mick with annoyance. "I intend to, fella." He turned to Geri and held out an old necklace. "How much for this, Geri?"

"They're all marked," Geri said in a businesslike way. She'd never particularly liked the sheriff, who was a bully and reputed to be a lecher. If he was picking up jewelry for his wife, it was probably to atone for a sin. More likely, he was picking up a trinket to give to his latest girlfriend.

To Geri's annoyance, her mother piped it with, "But of course, ten off to you, Sheriff."

Reston tucked the necklace into his shirt pocket. reached into a pants pocket and produced several bills from a wad held by a silver money clip. Mrs. Sanders accepted the money, but then returned one bill to him. "Jim, that's not right'."

Reston pushed her hand back. "That's for the tax," he grinned, flashing a row of perfect white teeth. Mrs. Sanders shrugged and accepted the bonus. "Now," Reston said to Geri, "if you'll kindly show me the way?"

"Give my regards to Julia, Jim," Mrs. Sanders said naively. Geri made a face which, luckily, the sheriff didn't see.

Geri and Mick followed the sheriff's blue police car to the Beardsly place. "Where is it?" the sheriff asked. stretching his long frame as he got out of his car.

"Around the side," Geri said, clutching Mick's hand for comfort.

The sheriff looked skeptically at them and saved a lingering look of malice for Mick, then ambled with his virile gait to the back of the house, followed by Mick and Geri.

Geri pointed to the spot where the skeleton had been. The ground was freshly turned, as it had been before.

But there was no skeleton there. None at all. Not so much as a bone.

Reston took a deep breath and seemed to be counting to ten to control his rage. Then he cast his icy blue-eyed glare on Mick. "Listen, fella, I don't know what you're up to but you're sure as hell not going to pull this bull around Fly Creek." He stepped closer to Mick, staring him in the eye almost nose to nose, Mick refused to be interrupted, and stood his ground as the sheriff growled, "I want you the hell out of this town."

It's hard to say what would have happened if Geri hadn't interceded. "But it was right here, Mr. Reston. We both saw it."

Reston relaxed a little. "Geri, now that's enough," he said with paternal tenderness to the girl he'd known since she'd been an infant. "I'd expect this kind of bull from your sister, but not you. Your father used to be real proud of you. If he were still alive and saw you now, he'd tan your fanny."

Mick was outraged. "She didn't do anything." The sheriff ignored him.

"I'm gonna let this go because it's too hot and I'm too busy to book this little city weasel. I've got a town to put back together."

He pivoted and walked purposefully back to his car, but abruptly stopped and whirled to point a threatening finger at Mick.

"If I even see you one more time, fella, you won't be able to call a city lawyer. 'Cause all the phones are dead."

They watched him climb into his car, which rumbled into life and roared out of the driveway with a shower of gravel.

Mick and Geri looked at each other, utterly confused and mystified, then turned back to the fresh earth. There was absolutely nothing there, nothing but a matchbook. Mick picked it up, studied it, shrugged and put it in his pocket.

"I just don't understand it," Geri sighed. "It didn't just walk away."

Mick looked around the woods. He didn't understand it any better than she did. Mick pulled a cigarette out of its pack and took out his butane lighter. He flicked it a few times but it was still damp and refused to burst into flame. "Got a light?" he asked Geri.

"I don't smoke," she said.

He remembered the matchbook he'd just picked up, and picked out a match that didn't look as if it would fall apart on the first strike. To his delight, it caught flame. "Son of a gun," he said, returning the matchbook to his top pocket.

They returned to the car; "But whose skeleton was it?" Geri mused, shutting the door and turning the ignition.

"Might have been from the revolutionary war for all we know," Mick said, keeping his doubts to himself for fear of alarming Geri. "It takes a body a long time to rot down to a clean skeleton. When I was a kid I dug up my dog that we'd buried in the back yard. I thought it would be a skeleton but it wasn't. I threw up."

On that happy note they returned to Geri's home, and the prospect of fresh clothes at last.

Chapter Seven

The attic smelled musty, and its poor insulation raised the temperature up there to broiling. Light filtering through a transom illuminated the clouds of dust thrown up by Mick as he rummaged through the trunk.

A red checkered flannel shirt struck his fancy and he hauled it out, holding it up. Though scarcely the sort of' thing he'd ordinarily wear, it did have a certain appeal.

If you're going to go rural, dress as the rurals do.

Alma Sanders, straddled in undignified adolescence over an old loveseat, shook her head and made a face that left no doubt about her reaction.

"That's not all too groovy," she said, suppressing a guffaw. "Unless you want to blend in with the creekers."

"What's a creeker?" Mick asked, holding the shirt up to his chest and modeling it for her.

"Fly Creek people. Very un-hip." To demonstrate her hipness, she reached into the cleavage of her wrap around blouse and produced a thin joint rolled in canary yellow paper. Mick looked at her with faint disapproval. He wasn't prudish about grass, but he wondered if perhaps Alma was a little too young for it.

"Smoking in Fly Creek is a bust," she commented, fingering the thin yellow tube and running it under her nose. "Did you meet Sheriff Reston yet?" The thought of Sheriff Reston sent the kid into near hysterics. "Just too far out for words. Got a match?"

"Uh, yeah. Yeah, I do." Mick said, remembering the soggy matchbook he'd picked up behind Beardsly's house. He reached into the top pocket of his shirt and handed them to Alma "Keep 'em," he said. He looked into the trunk some more and was about to rummage deeper when he felt an itch on his leg. This was the second time he'd felt it, and he scratched it heavily.

Alma was studying the matchbook. "Quigley's. Oh wow, have you been' there?" Mick grunted a negative. He'd become quite preoccupied with his itch, to the point of rolling up his pants leg to inspect the area, which was an angry red with a number of welts.

"Quigley's is a piss," Alma said, lighting up her joint and taking a deep, sibilant hit on it. "I go there with some of my friends. wrecked out of our gourds," she continued, holding the smoke in her lungs. "We just order tequila and watch the old farts drink themselves into a stupor."

She handed the joint to Mick, who took a hit on it himself, but seemed more preoccupied with his itch than with getting high.

"How long has that been itching like that?" asked Alma.

"It just started." He gestured at the matchbook in Alma's hands. "What about Beardsly? The antique guy? Does he go to Quigley's?"

Alma found this so funny she burst into a fit of smokey coughing. "Go there? He lives there. Aaron Beardsly is a stoned cold alkie."

Mick exhaled the smoke, savoring the high quality of. the grass. Somehow it surprised him to find grass smoked down here, though why, he wasn't sure. He shrugged and went back to the trunk, and hauled out a blue shirt that wasn't too bad.

When he looked up, Alma was gazing at his chest with an interest that made him uncomfortable.

"You must really have a thing for Geri, to come all the way down here from the city," she observed.

'I'm trying to cram my whole summer vacation into a few days," he answered.

"So I heard."

He donned the shirt and shrugged. If it wasn't that great, it wasn't that bad either. "It's sure nice to get away from the city," he said in a pleasant, conversation tone.

Alma offered him another toke, but Mick declined. Alma burrowed back into her blouse and came up with another joint, giving it to Mick. "Save it for later," she said, smiling pixieishly.

"Why's that?"

"That stuff on your leg," she laughed. "It's poison ivy."

Through the mellow buzz in her head Alma heard a horn honking. That was probably Jeff, Eddie, and Susanne, who'd said they might be going down to Quigley's to drink and would pick her up if they did. She took the stairs two at a time and peered out the screen door. Yes, there was Jeff at the wheel of his vintage Buick convertible, with long-haired Susanne squeezed between him and Eddie. They greeted their friend, and Eddie climbed into the back seat to sit with Alma.

The car took off for town, and Alma had no sooner climbed in than she was telling her gang all about her sister's boyfriend Mick. If Alma loved anything in the world, it was gossip.

Quigley's was surprisingly crowded for this time of day. The four teenagers attributed it to the fact that with the town's electricity down, people wanted to go someplace where there were other people—and cold beer on tap. Still, it was pretty hot in there, and after ordering their drinks they fell into a state of semi somnolence. Luckily, their friend Amy walked by the window of the bar, carrying her transistor radio. They practically shanghaied her, not so much because they liked her as because she had a radio. The blast of rock music annoyed some of the more sedate patrons, but at least it livened things up in there.

"I'll bet there's gonna be a big rise in population in

Fly Creek nine months from now," Alma shouted, remembering what had happened in New York City nine months after the big blackout back in 1965.

"Yeah," said Jeff. "With no electricity tonight there's gonna be nothing else to do." He gazed with calf like eyes at Susanne, the meaning of his expression plain to read. Susanne looked at him blankly, pretending not to understand.

They peered through the grimy window of the bar, seeking grist for their giggly gossip-mill, and found a perfect target in Sheriff Reston, who'd just emerged from Town Hall, a tall, dark-haired woman in her late thirties attached to his arm. They couldn't tell who she was, but who she was *not* was Reston's wife, that was for damn sure, and they had a Class-A giggle over that one.

"Uh-oh," said Amy, "looks like Big Jim is at it again."

"I've gotta hand it to that guy," said Eddie. "He knows how to take advantage of a situation. His wife's away visiting her mother. Big storm hits, roads ·are all flooded out, no chance of her popping in on him. No phones..." He eyed Sheriff Reston's "escort" as they crossed the street, apparently heading for Quigley's, he wore a cool looking white outfit that could not, it was plain to see, have come from any city closer than Atlanta. She was probably a stranded tourist, which for Sheriff Reston was like a lamb to a hungry wolf.

"What I don't understand is what those chicks see in him," said Jeff.

"I wonder where he's gonna take her tonight," Alma mused.

"You mean take her, or *take* her?" Jeff guffawed. priding himself in the subtlety of his *double entendres.*

"Both," said Susanne, and they all laughed.

Sheriff Reston entered the bar with his lady friend and looked over at the five kids, squinting at the glasses on the table to make sure there was nothing more potent in them than Coke. There wasn't. What was potent was the flask of Wild Turkey secreted in Jeff's pants pocket.

Reston sat down at the table nearest the bar and asked for the luncheon menu, and the five kids went back to their people watching.

"There's the dude from New York," Alma said excitedly. The other four peered intently out of the window to study the pleasant looking but somewhat scholarly young man strolling through town with Geri. They weren't sure what they'd expected, but *it* sure hadn't been someone who wore glasses.

As they studied Mick, Roger Grimes entered the tavern and plopped heavily onto a stool. Mr. Quigley, a thin, almost wizened, red-faced man, looked up from the newspaper he'd spread on the bar and asked Roger what he wanted to drink. Roger asked for a double bourbon, neat. Not even a chaser. Quigley looked questioningly at Roger, then did as he'd been told. He'd known Roger since the boy had come of drinking age, and he knew that Willie Grimes' son hit the booze pretty hard whenever he was upset. He also knew that Roger had a tendency to destroy the bar and anyone who tried to restrain him when he got into these moods. He poured one shot of bourbon into a glass, then cut it with another shot of water, hoping Roger wouldn't see or taste the difference. He'd done this before for Roger or other troublemakers, and though technically, he supposed. he was cheating his customers, Quigley did it for only the very best of motives—to protect his bar, and to protect a man on the rampage from hurting himself.

At least it was comforting to know Sheriff Reston was here.

As Roger downed half his drink in one gulp, Geri came into the bar hand-in-hand with a young man that Mr. Quigley did not recognize. At once it became clear to Quigley what the source of Roger's misery was, for Quigley knew that Roger was sweet on Geri Sanders, and it must be quite a blow to him to see her taking up with this new beau. Quigley had to admit it was a little hard to see what Geri saw in this new young man, who looked like a lawyer on vacation. (Joe Quigley had lived a long time, and there was little about people he didn't know or couldn't figure out.) On the other hand, Quigley could also understand why, Geri didn't really cotton that much to Roger, who was, as the local expression had it, just a mite touched.

One thing you could say about this new young man, though: he wasn't above coming right up to his rival and saying hello to him. He dropped down onto the stool next to Roger and put his hand on the sulking boy's shoulder. "Hey, Roger," he said cheerfully.

Roger shrugged off the hand like a cow shuddering off a horsefly.

Mick shrugged and turned to Geri, who'd just slid onto the barstool beside him. "Hi, Mr. Quigley," she said, ordering a beer.

"Excuse me, sir," Mick said to the man behind the bar, "but we're looking for Aaron Beardsly. Has he been around?"

"Aaron? No. I ain't seen Aaron since last night. He left just before it really started coming down."

Roger shifted uncomfortably in his seat at the mention of Beardsly's name, but no one connected this with the puzzling disappearance of the antiques dealer.

"Geri, everything all right at your place?" Mr. Quigley asked. "Mom okay?"

"Fine," said Geri, swallowing some beer and sighing contentedly.

"Say, that was one heck of a storm, wasn't it?" the tavern owner said. "I hear the electricity'll be out till tomorrow morning." Mick and Geri nodded. For a moment there was an awkward silence as Mr. Quigley stared penetratingly at Mick. Then he leaned closer and said, "You people antique shopping? Well, you look like a nice enough fella. Let me give you a little tip."

The old man put his hand on Mick's shoulder. "Stay away

from ol' Aaron. He's 'a little, um, steep. Now, I have a garage filled with the most beautiful stuff you ever saw."

To demonstrate, he reached down and produced a rust-laden brass diver's helmet, the glass mask scratched. the neck rim dented.

"Why, in New York, you'd have to pay..."

Geri interrupted him before he could get deeper into his sales pitch. "Uh, Mr. Quigley, we'll stop in if we have time. If you see Mr. Beardsly..."

The old man didn't seem to be overly offended by their sales resistance. "Oh, he'll be here tonight, you can rest assured on that."

Mick started to push away from the bar, but Roger looked so morose that in spite of Roger's rejection of Mick's first gesture, the young m n felt he had to make another effort. "Listen, 'm really sorry about those worms."

"Just forget it," Roger said, not looking up from his drink.

"We're going fishing," Mick said brightly, hoping this would lure the guy out of his mood. "I'd really like you to join us. You must know all the best spots."

Roger shook his head again. Then Geri leaned across Mick and touched Roger fondly on the wrist. "Oh, come on, Roger, it'll be better if you stay away from your father for a little while."

The boy's resistance started to crumble. Smiling weakly at Geri, he said, "When are you going?"

"Soon as we finish lunch," Geri beamed. "About an hour."

Roger shrugged indifferently, but they could see the temptation was overcoming the lad. "I'll have to pick up some stuff at the bait shop," he finally said to their delight. "I'll meet you down by the boats."

"Great!" said Mick. "You can show how to use the new reel I bought."

They climbed down from the stools and were about to walk out when they noticed Alma and her friends seated at the table.

They greeted each other. Alma's friends, after the introductions, studied Mick indifferently.

"What are you drinkin'?" Eddie asked him.

"Nothing, thanks. We're just trying to track down Aaron Beardsly."

"Hey, yeah," Eddie said. "I hear you're into antiques. I have a dynamite old Nazi bayonet that you might be interested in doing a deal on."

"Sounds interesting," Mick said politely.

"You can come to my house and take a look at it," Eddie pressed.

"Uh, not now. Geri and I are going fishing."

"Well then, maybe tonight? We'll all be here. I'll bring it with me. The candlelight won't do it justice, but what can you do?"

Growing quite uncomfortable, Mick muttered some cordial platitude and made his escape.

Geri drove him back to her house, where she made tuna sandwiches. She gobbled hers down while Mick applied calamine lotion to his still itchy leg. "You'll find that everybody in Fly Creek considers himself an antique dealer," she said. "Nobody throws anything away. You never know what the tourists want."

Mick got up, dried his hands on a piece of paper towel, and stole up behind Geri. Kissing her on the back of the neck, he whispered, "Guess what this tourist wants?"

Geri giggled, yielded a moment, then ducked away. "Tuna fish will have to do for now."

Mick sighed and sat down at the table, tackling his sandwich. It tasted distinctly inferior to Geri's neck.

"That reminds me. Where do I sleep?" he asked.

"In the extra room."

His face sank into his sandwich. Then he brightened again. "Maybe I'll sneak up to your room."

"My mother would have a fit."

"She'd never see me. It'll be dark *as* hell." He caressed Geri's back for emphasis.

Geri's breath quickened. "Better if I sneak down. You'd probably bang into something and wake everybody up."

Mick smiled and gazed dreamily at his sandwich. "Looks good."

It's hard to say where this smoldering exchange would have led had Mrs. Sanders not come into the kitchen. She began opening cupboards and drawers and setting out pots, pans, and a variety of utensils for what appeared to be a king-sized dinner. At one point she removed an electric knife from an appliance cabinet, then realized it would do her absolutely no good without electricity. She made a face, returned it to the cabinet, and took a conventional carving knife out of a utility drawer and began sharpening it by hand.

"Don't fill yourselves up too much. I'm making a big roast tonight. I want you to be hungry by seven o'clock." She silently thanked her stars that their oven worked on gas instead of electricity. Many a family in Fly Creek would be dining on sandwiches tonight.

"Don't bother with a roast, Mrs. Sanders," Mick said. "We'll catch enough fish for dinner."

Mrs. Sanders never missed an opportunity, even when her daughter's chosen boyfriend *was* sitting a few feet. away. "Geri, why don't you ask Roger over for dinner tonight? He worked so hard cleaning up those branches."

Geri thought it over and said, "Sure, Mom." Anything she could do to ingratiate Roger again after the disaster of the missing worms would be a plus. Besides, after Mick returned to New York City, she'd need Roger to take her to dances and picnics.

Geri and Mick ate their sandwiches in silence, mooning at each other while Mrs. Sanders puttered in the kitchen. Then Geri raised a question she'd been meaning to ask Mick. "Do you suppose something happened to Mr. Beardsly?"

"Probably not. I'll bet we see him tonight boozing it up in a dark corner at Quigley's."

"Do you really plan on going there?"

"Sure. I can't disappoint the guy with the bayonet," he laughed. Bayonets were not really Mick's idea of antiques, but he didn't see much he could do to get out of his promise to Alma's friend without offending him. Offend him and he'd offend Alma, and Mick didn't want to alienate anyone in Geri's family.

Geri opened the refrigerator and took out some milk. Despite the block of ice—or perhaps because of it, since it had diminished to the size of a fist and didn't look effective enough to cool a glass of water—the milk container was not very cold. She poured out two glasses and handed one to Mick.

Mick raised the glass to his lips, then remembered something and lowered it, looking a little sallow.

"There was a worm in my egg cream," he announced flatly.

"What?"

"When I went into that luncheonette," Mick explained to Geri, whose eyes bugged with horror, "I ordered an egg cream, and I found a worm in it."

Mick stared into the glass of milk, wondering not just about this one but about all the milk he would ever drink, or never drink, again.

"What's an egg cream?" Geri asked, apparently as much put off by the obnoxious sounding name of the drink as by the fact that there had been a worm in it.

"It's like a chocolate..." Mick wandered off into some private reflection. "I wonder if it was my fault after all. Maybe it had something to do with the truckload."

Geri seemed utterly bewildered, but not so bewildered that she was able to finish her milk. She got up, looking faintly nauseated, and left the house with Mick. Mrs. Sanders was appalled that the two young people had left full glasses of milk, and carefully poured them back into the container.

Looking cautiously around the Grimes property, Mick and Geri ventured toward the truck whose cargo (or lack of it) had been the cause of so much unhappiness.

"Is Roger around?" Mick said, feeling a little anxious about this snooping. Mick was well built and athletic, if a bit slight, but there was no doubt who'd be the loser in a test of belligerence with Roger, who'd done nothing but manual labor all his life.

"He's probably at the dock getting the boat ready," Geri whispered. She wasn't concerned with Roger so much as with Roger's father. Neighbors or not, he wouldn't hesitate to thrash Geri if he found her trespassing and tampering with the truck.

Mick turned the handle on the back doors of the truck and pulled them open. A vile gust of urea and putrefaction overwhelmed him momentarily, and again he shook his head and asked himself what kind of people farm worms.

He peered into the darkness and made out very little except for a few shovels and mud rakes. But there wasn't a worm to be seen. Not so much as a single one. Or even half of one, which to Mick's way of thinking was twice as disgusting as a whole one.

There was one thing that interested him, though: a rolled-up tarpaulin sack resting on a shelf on the side of the truck. It was too far away for him to reach from the ground, so he shinnied himself up and ventured into the foul black interior, whose floor was slimy beneath his shoes.

He tugged lightly at the tarpaulin, and when it released its contents, it was all Mick could do to keep from passing out. It was the skeleton. It slid out of the tarpaulin and landed with a clattering of bones at Mick's feet.

"The skeleton!" Geri gasped. "How'd it get there?"

"Yeah," said Mick, "*if* it's the same one. They all look alike to me."

Suddenly, remembering something he'd read in a detective novel once, he took the skull in his hands and tried to twist it off the vertebrae that attached it to the skeleton's spine. But a thick layer of gristly cartilage held it firmer than he'd expected.

Before he could go further, Geri hissed. Someone was coming! He covered the bones and jumped off the truck. The moment his feet touched ground Geri shut the doors of the truck and prodded Mick around the truck's side. Mick was confused for a second, then looked at the Grimes house and realized what Geri was doing. Grimes himself had just stepped out of the back door carrying a can of garbage. Looking at the truck, he noticed that its back doors were slightly ajar. He put the can down and ambled to the truck, muttering curses to himself about the goddamn worms learning how to pry crates loose and open truck doors by themselves.

With Mick and Geri a bare yard from him, crouched behind a rear tire, Grimes peered inside the truck, muttered a few more oaths, and slammed the doors shut, closing them securely with a sharp twist of the handle. Then he walked back to the garbage can, filling the air with his low opinion of worms, trucks, and life in general.

Mick and Geri got to their feet. "Let's tell Sheriff Reston," Geri said.

"Tell him what?" Mick said despairingly. Two encounters with that sonofabitch had been two more than Mick needed, thank you. Reston would probably accuse him of grave-robbing or some such and keep his promise of throwing Mick in jail and tossing away the key. "If 'we only knew whose bones those are," he mused. But he'd already formulated a plan, and as they drove down to Fly Creek Lagoon, Mick told Geri what it was.

Chapter Eight

They parked on the grass and walked about a hundred yards to the dock where Roger was kneeling, un tying the painter that secured a wooden rowboat to a mooring cleat.

Mick paused before they got there and reminded Geri what the strategy was. "Remember what I told you. I'll need at least a half hour. Do anything you can to keep Roger out on the lake. We'll meet back at the house."

Geri dug her fingernails into his arm. "Mick, you've got me scared."

"Welcome to the club," Mick gulped.

Roger waved a greeting and Mick reciprocated, looking around and inhaling the fresh salty tang mingled with a less pleasant odor of slimy mud and rotting fish. The lagoon itself was a quiet backwater covered with moss and other floating vegetation, but beyond it was the bay opening to the sea, a glorious sight. A column of pink clouds soared on the horizon, and in the near distance flocks of gulls shrieked and squabbled over the corpses of fish washed ashore in last night's storm. It was that that had made Mick wrinkle up his nose.

They climbed into the boat, which shimmied precariously as they distributed their fishing gear and their weight.

Roger took the oars and pulled into the glass-smooth lagoon effortlessly, his biceps rippling as the boat sliced a green swath through the mossy surface.

Roger raised his face to the sun. Geri removed her blouse. revealing a halter top on which two pairs of male eyes fixed admiringly. She rolled up the cuffs of her short jeans to give her thighs a chance to absorb some sun. For a moment Roger almost lost control of the boat.

He finally maneuvered the little craft into a spoon-shaped area near a half-fallen tree, then set the oars inside the boat. Looking with some distaste at Mick, he found him peeling the price tag off his fishing reel. What this dude's appeal to Geri was, Roger reflected, he'd never know.

Roger reached down and handed Geri her rod, then pulled a sharp-bladed fishing knife from his pants pocket and cut the ends of the lines, attached lengths of transparent blue leader, then tied on hooks and sinkers while Mick, the complete fisherman, applied suntan lotion and insect repellent to his exposed skin. He offered some to Geri and Roger, but they laughed—Geri amusedly, Roger disgustedly—and declined.

Mick sniffed a deep draught of air into his lungs. "Nothing like fresh, salt air," he said. Then he wrinkled his nose and gave in to the temptation to do his Groucho routine. Hunching his shoulders and tapping the ash off an imaginary cigar. Mick added, "And that's nothing like fresh, salt air."

Geri laughed. Roger shook his head and shifted his weight uncomfortably, praying for some good fishing so he wouldn't have to listen to this clown for the next few hours. Jesus, the guy couldn't even open the blades of his brand new multipurpose camping knife and had to give it to Geri, who pried a blade open with her long nails. This New York City jerk would probably survive in the wilderness for about a half hour, Roger said to himself, adding that the temptation was strong to take him out there to prove it.

"What's that smell?" asked Mick.

"Low tide," Geri explained. "This water is too polluted to swim in." She gazed into the brown. mossy water. "I don't know how the fish stay alive."

Roger decided to prove that Mick wasn't the only one who could make jokes. "Maybe they come from New York," he said. Geri burst into laughter; it was one of the few funny things Roger had ever said. Mick, for some reason, found it less than hilarious.

Mick reached for a cardboard box. It had a wire handle and reminded him of the kind of box you bring home from a Chinese take-out restaurant. Hell, nothing could have made him happier at this moment than to open it and find a mound of lobster Cantonese or *egg foo yung*. Having set himself up with these enchanting fantasies, his plunge to the depths of disgust was that much more devastating when he opened the lid and looked inside. The world seemed to sway before his eyes, and he was certain he was going to puke.

One worm, even in an egg cream, was nauseating enough. A box full of them, writhing like a nest of disturbed rattlesnakes, was more than any human should be asked to take, especially when that human had been thinking about lobster Cantonese and *egg foo yung* just a moment before. He shut the lid immediately, and though Mick's face was ordinarily pale, it seemed to go six shades paler still.

Trying to maintain his cool, he passed the box to Roger with a hearty laugh. "Hey, Roger, you're a pro at this. I don't want to waste time trying to get them on the hook." Indeed, the notion of trying to drive a hook through that purple segmented body was enough to make Mick swear off fish to the end of his days.

Roger took the box in hand with a cocky nod of the head, but then something strange happened. Roger turned pale. He turned pale and broke into a perspiration that did not, to Mick's observation, have anything to do with the heat of the day. He fumbled with the lid of the box, and Mick noticed his hands were actually trembling. Roger peeked inside, his eyes widened, his lip curled, and he slammed the lid shut.

"I can't!" Roger whimpered. "I can't! Oh God, they're disgusting."

His two friends gaped at him as if he'd just turned into a zebra.

"Roger, I don't understand," Mick said. "Don't you handle worms all the time? I mean, a worm farm and all?"

"I hate it," Roger said through clenched teeth. "Dad always made me touch them. I can't even stand to look at them." He seemed to be on the verge of crying.

Mick shook his head in disbelief, not knowing whether to laugh or cry himself.

All at once Roger's hand darted out and clutched Mick's arm in a death grip. Roger's eyes were glazed and bulged out of their sockets. His nostrils flared, and his lips slavered with spittle. "The worms are everywhere," he shouted. "Millions and millions and millions of crawling, slimy, squirming, disgusting—"

"ROGER!" Geri's voice barked out across the lagoon, silencing a chorus of tree toads and crickets, and sending a flock of seagulls thundering into the sky, screaming abuse at the humans who had disturbed their feeding.

At the sound of Geri's command, Roger slumped and relaxed and appeared to return to normal. Whatever fantasy had taken possession of his imagination drained back into the hideous recesses of his tortured mind. He took a deep breath and even managed a nervous, apologetic laugh.

Geri decided that if two strong males couldn't stand the sight of worms, she'd have to show them there was at least one healthy human being in the boat. She picked up the box herself, opened the top, and removed one from the turbulent mass of plum-colored flesh that had quickened its agitated writhing when the sunlight struck it directly. Removing one worm from a pack was easier said than done, for the two or three dozen creatures in the box had wrapped themselves into a knot that even Alexander's sword might not have severed.

The mass reacted to Geri's patient untangling by writhing like a swarm of disturbed bees. Angry little fangs bared themselves, but the adept girl managed to avoid their probes. At the same time, she remarked to herself that she'd never seen worms so angry and aggressive. It was very puzzling.

She removed a specimen about four inches long, held it by the neck, and struggled with it as it tried to wrap its body and tail around her finger like some miniature python. When the barbed hook she held in her left hand penetrated its side, sliced up inside its entrails, and emerged out of its neck the creature gave a convulsion of frightening strength, causing Geri to toss the baited hook overboard instinctively to protect her fingers. An involuntary shiver rippled down her spine.

Trying not to show her fear, she baited Roger's hook as coolly as she could. Again, the worm she chose resisted her prying fingertips violently, and it was all she could do to avoid the two fangs which, tiny as they were, seemed capable of doing tremendous damage.

A glance in Roger's direction revealed a boy torn between shame and fear. He sat at the oars, head hung on his chest, rocking back and forth. But had she asked him to bait his own hook, she feared he would burst out all over again into fits of hysterics.

Meanwhile, Mick had been so embarrassed by his display of faintheartedness that he'd plunged into the box and hauled out a worm—the smallest one he could find, admittedly, but it was still technically a worm—and was trying to maneuver it onto his hook. He held book and worm at arm's length, looking like some nearsighted grannie trying to thread a needle.

Geri giggled and Mick looked over at her, disappointed with himself. This was a perfect opportunity to win points in his rivalry with Roger for Geri's affection but be was blowing it.

Geri threw him an affectionate look that said, Clumsy and chickenhearted as you are, I love you anyway.

That wasn't good enough for Mick and be determined to take the bull by the horns, or in this case the worm by the neck.

Unfortunately, while he was looking at Geri, the worm took him by the finger instead. It took it in its two fangs and not only bit its soft flesh but burrowed the tip of his head under it in the same instant.

Mick felt an excruciating pain as if someone had punctured his fingertip with a pencil and then inserted the pencil an inch deep. Mick howled with agony and jumped to his feet, almost capsizing the boat.

He now did what he had not been able to do: took the worm by the neck just behind the head and pulled it firmly out of its burrow in his finger. The pain of taking it out was as searing as the pain of its entrance, but at least it was out. He threw it on the floor of the boat and stomped it. The heel of his shoe spliced the worm in half, crushing its head with a popping noise that squirted blood and pulpy guts over the bottom of the boat.

The other half of the worm spasmed and flailed across the floor of the boat, heading toward Geri. All this happened in mere moments, but it seemed like hours. Geri picked her feet up and sat on the thwart like a kitchen maid who's seen a mouse.

Mick deliberately followed the tail of the worm across the bottom of the boat with his heel, remembering vividly that the tails of worms will regenerate a head. No thanks, he said to himself, bringing his heel down on the tail and putting all 175 of his pounds into the effort of slaying this thing which could not have weighed more than an ounce. Again it made a popping sound, its intestine exploding like a balloon.

Mick collapsed on the thwart, panting and trembling, sucking on his bleeding finger.

"Mick? Are you okay?" Geri was crying. "What happened?"

"The little mother bit me. Jesus Christ."

Geri took his hand and examined it. "Are you sure it wasn't the hook?"

By comparison the hook would have been as tender as kiss. "Geri, the thing bit right into my hand." Recalling what she'd told him earlier, he added, "I guess I held the wrong end."

She examined the wound closely, shaking her head. No, a fishhook assuredly did not make that kind of wound. "They don't usually bite hard enough to penetrate the skin. I never saw one bite like that."

"I did, once." It was Roger speaking. His eyes were fixed blankly on the horizon, like some shell-shocked soldier after a battle. He spoke like one in a dream, in a coma. "When I was small, Dad would experiment with different ways of getting worms out of the ground. One day he tried electricity."

Mick and Geri leaned forward to hear Roger's almost inaudible voice as he related the incident that had traumatized him almost twenty years ago. He recalled vividly the outbuilding his father had converted into an experimental station, the fishtank: filled with soil, the electrical contacts with the alligator clips....

"Did it work?" Mick asked.

"Yeah. It got them out of the ground." he said matter-of-factly. Then he held up his hand.

Half of his thumb was missing.

Mick and Geri stared at it, totally aghast.

"He had to cut most of my thumb to get it off," Roger said.

Geri felt tears springing involuntarily into her eyes. She'd noticed Roger's deformity years ago, of course, but had never had the temerity to ask him how it had happened. But of the many possibilities she had ruminated about, it had never occurred to her that it could have been a worm. "Roger, I never knew..."

Roger shrugged. "That's okay. It ain't no big deal."

The attention of all three focused on the box of worms. "Where did you get those from?" Geri asked, shuddering.

"From the farm," Roger replied.

"Listen," Mick said, pulling a handkerchief out of his pants pocket and wrapping it around his finger, "I want to get back and put something on this. Why don't you drop me off on shore."

"We'll all go," said Geri.

Mick threw her some eye signals, hoping Roger wouldn't catch them. She and Mick had agreed that Mick would separate from them on some pretext or another, and the worm-bite was a perfect one—though he'd have preferred one a little more innocuous. In the excitement Geri had forgotten the scenario, but now she remembered as Mick said, "No, no, I want to catch a nap anyway. Let's see if you two can land some fish for dinner."

Geri looked deeply distressed at being left alone with Roger. "Mick, I really don't..."

"Come on Geri," Mick assured her with a smile. "Roger will keep you company, won't you, Rog?" Mick didn't realize that that was exactly what was bothering Geri.

Roger, thrilled to be rid of this intruder, rowed vigorously to the shore. Mick leaped out onto the muddy bank and trudged back to where they'd come from while Roger smartly turned the rowboat around and stroked it into the lagoon.

Chapter Nine

Roger hauled the dripping oars into the boat and let it drift to a halt in the middle of the lagoon. They gazed at the shore, watching the figure of Mick recede into the woods. Then he was gone, and they were completely alone. Just Geri and Roger and a box of worms.

"Might as well try right here," Roger said, peering into the murky water. "One place is as good *as* another, I guess."

Geri didn't agree. She'd rather, a million times more, be on dry land with Mick than in a boat in the middle of nowhere with this unstable young man. She prayed he'd keep to his fishing and give her no trouble.

She picked up her rod and cast her line into a quiet patch of water a few yards astern of the rowboat. It made a plop as the sinker punctured the surface of the lagoon, then no sound was heard. She gazed at the point where her line cleaved the water, waiting for a tug, but she soon became aware of Roger's eyes roving over her body. She concentrated harder, pretending nonchalantly that the boy's hungry gaze did not exist.

Finally, she became terribly uncomfortable. "You want me to bait one up for you?" she asked. "Two lines are better than one."

"No thanks," Roger said. "I'm fine."

They sat this way for several minutes, almost frozen into their postures like the subjects of a seascape. There was no breeze, not a ripple on the surface of the lagoon. Roger remained fixed on the bow thwart, oars in hand, looking at Geri; Geri remained fixed on the stern thwart, looking at the water. Nothing moved.

Nothing but the worms.

For, unknown to Geri and Roger, the lid of the box had come undone when Mick had jumped to his feet and rocked the boat. The worms, fearful of sunlight, had at first shrunk back into their seething tangle in the box, but a half dozen specimens, tortured by a hunger they had never known before, had ventured out of the box and slithered out, dropping to the floor of the boat. They probed the metal bottom angrily, seeking cool dirt and food, but all they could see, smell, and sense were the trunk-like objects that rested on the floor of the boat.

Those were human feet.

And they made for them. Slowly, but certainly, and, to the owners of those feet, invisibly.

Suddenly this frozen portrait was shattered as Geri's rod bowed downward, its tip quivering violently. "I got one!" she cried joyously, standing up. She handled it well, her arms straining to keep the line tight as she played the fish closer to the boat, reeling in line as it went slack "Roger, Roger, it's a big one!" she shouted. Roger whooped triumphantly and stood up behind her, trying to catch a glimpse of the fish as the shuddering line made irregular circles closer and closer to the boat. At last it was close enough to pull out. Steadying himself by placing one arm around Geri's waist, he reached over the gunwale and yanked the line. A porgy splashed out of the depths, flapping angrily.

Holding the squirming fish in his left hand, Roger worked at the hook, trying to remove it, but it was lodged deep in the fish's throat. Roger had never been one for patience and subtle finesse. He simply tugged brutally. The hook ripped through the cartilage of the fish's mouth, spattering blood on Roger's wrist.

He grinned sadistically as he grasped the fish firmly and dipped it into the water to wash it, then passed a line through its gill and secured it. Geri leaned over Roger to get another look at her catch.

"Think he's big enough for dinner?" she asked. "He's a big one, all right."

Geri was uncomfortable alone with Roger, but Mick had told her to stall for time. "Maybe we should go for one more," she said. There was still enough worm covering the barb of the hook so that she wouldn't have to bait it again.

"It's all right with me," said Roger, understating the case considerably. As Geri cast a second time, Roger snuggled up close to her. "You know, Geri," he said, "this is the first time we've ever been alone together. It's nice, isn't it? Just the two of us."

Geri felt herself freezing up. She smiled plastically, holding it on her face like an entrant in the Miss America contest.

"Geri?"

"Mmm?"

"Are you staying in the same room with him tonight?" Roger asked.

"You should know better than to listen to Alma," Geri said, scolding him mildly.

Roger let out a breath of relief. "I wish…I wish we could have done this before he came up here."

"I'm enjoying it too, Roger," Geri said. She tried to infuse the statement with enough warmth to sound sincere, but not so much as to give Roger the wrong impression.

"Geri," he announced, more talkative than she'd ever seen him, "I've been thinking. With your dad gone and all, well…"

Oh no, Geri cried silently to herself, don't get serious, Roger, please don't!

"I've been thinking you need someone to help run the business, moving heavy furniture and all. I'm ready to tell Pop that I don't want to take over the farm."

Geri's mind raced ahead, seeking the proper phrasing for declining his offer without hurting or enraging him. With Roger it was usually one or the other.

Before he could press the question upon her, he said, "By the way, Geri, I have a surprise for you."

"Really?" she asked, shuddering slightly. "What is it?"

"I told you. A surprise."

He reached behind her and jiggled her fishing rod. With the instinct of a born fisherwoman, Geri snapped her wrist to set the hook in the fish's mouth. The sudden movement tipped the boat and Roger saw his opportunity. He grabbed her by the back of the head and pulled her face to his, pressing his mouth over hers with a violent, animal passion. His other hand wrapped firmly around her waist and entrapped her in a vise-like grip.

"Roger, please! Stop it!" she managed to cry beneath the crush of Roger's hungry lips.

But Roger wouldn't let go, and her resistance only enflamed him. "It's him, isn't it? He comes down from. New York and takes over. Well, I'll kill him if he ever touches you again!"

Once more he pressed his lips to Geri's face and neck. His rough beard and hot breath nauseated her. She managed to wedge her fist between her body and his. Had they been on dry land she would have been no match for him, but the fact that they were in the boat equalized her chances, for he had to concern himself with rocking the boat and capsizing it. As the boat tipped the struggling couple at a precarious angle, Roger shifted his weight to compensate. That was what Geri had been hoping. She pushed him with all her might. He stumbled on one of the oars and fell on his face into the bottom of the boat.

Into the worms.

The last time the boat had tipped, the box had fallen to the floor, spilling the rest of the worms out of it. They separated from each other and scurried angrily in every direction. Then Roger fell upon them, crushing a number of them but only trapping many more who reacted as one might have expected.

They sank their teeth deep into the intruding mass of human flesh.

Which happened to belong to Roger's face.

Roger's scream was the most ghastly, unearthly sound Geri had ever heard. At first she didn't understand. Then, as Roger leaped to his feet, she saw.

At least a dozen worms had burrowed into his face.

One had punctured his cheek and was squirming into his mouth.

Another had penetrated his temple and was insinuating itself into his skull.

Still another had crawled under his eyelid. Still another had burrowed through his nose. There were two more *in* his chin.

And one inside his ear.

For a moment, as Roger struggled to his feet, he was incapable of self-defense. So enormous was his shock that he stood in the boat like a zombie, treating Geri to a sight so horrifying it would be the stuff of nightmares for the rest of her life. Worms were half buried in Roger's face, inching their way into the muscle and cartilage and brain beneath the skin.

Then Roger began to beat his face wildly, shrieking like a damned soul in the lowest ring of hell. He was absolutely mad with the agony of it, and Geri was paralyzed with fear and uncertainty. She didn't know how to begin helping Roger. Did she beat his face, cut the exposed ends of the worms off with a knife? At the moment she felt the best thing she could do would be to draw a knife across his throat, putting him out of his misery.

Before she could decide what to do, Roger tilted backward and capsized the boat. Still shrieking insanely, Roger half ran, half swam out of the lagoon and ran blindly into the woods.

Geri felt her feet touch firm ground and waded out of the

shallows onto dry land, running after Roger. She caught sight of him clawing at his face and grappling with the thick brush like a frenzied ape. "Roger! Roger!" she shouted, trying to keep sight of him. She dreaded what would become of him if he disappeared. His only hope was to let her help him.

But there was no hope. His insane pain had given him the strength of a dozen men, and he ripped into the woods with the stamina of a great beast. She called his name several times more but was answered only by the distant cry of the maddened boy.

She burst into sobs.

Chapter Ten

Mick surveyed the Grimes' property from the edge of the woods, then advanced like a guerrilla soldier, from tree to tree, stealthily. He looked around once more and, seeing no sign of Willie Grimes, dashed for the truck. Again, checking for signs of Roger's father, and finding none, he opened the doors of the truck and climbed in, shutting the doors behind him.

Once again, the stench nearly overwhelmed him, he managed to avoid it by breathing through his mouth. He waited a minute for his eyes to adjust to the darkness, but it was still black as pitch. He reached into his pocket for his butane lighter and flicked it a couple of times. It burst into a low orange flame, which he held above the dusty tarpaulin.

Hoping there would be no more surprises—but tensing his legs to spring the hell out of there if there were—he unwrapped the tarp. There was the skeleton, as he'd left it. Feeling somewhat like a fugitive from a voodoo ceremony, he began to twist the head off it, neck as he'd started to do before Mr. Grimes had interrupted him. It was as hot as a sauna in there, and the air was close and foul, and it was not easy to work on the head while holding his lighter in the other hand.

But at last, with a final mighty tug, Mick wrenched the head loose from the gristle that attached it to the spinal column. Placing the smooth, round skull under his shirt, he climbed out of the rear of the truck and into the bright sunlight.

"BUSTED!" a voice boomed.

Mick's heart flipped into his throat and he was about to raise his hands in a gesture of surrender when he recognized Alma.

"Hi," he said feebly, his voice cracking like a yodeler's. He held the skeleton under bis shirt as if by some miracle Alma wouldn't notice it.

No such luck.

"What you got there?"

Mick picked up his shirt tail and revealed the skull.

Alma tried to be cool, but if you'd asked her to guess what Mick had been hiding, a skull would have been the last thing to occur to her. "Ooow. Who is it?"

"That's what I want to find out."

"You got that out of Roger's truck? I don't think he'd dig that."

"I'll return it," Mick said sarcastically. He started to walk back into the woods.

"Okay if I come?" she said, skipping beside him.

Mick wanted to tell her to buzz off, but there was no way. "Sure," he sighed. "Why not?"

Mrs. Sanders finished preparations for dinner, feeling rather smug about having done it all without electricity. She was also feeling rather exhausted, since it had been years since she'd used mechanical means, rather than electric, to open cans, grate oranges for the dressing, and mash the sweet potatoes till they were as smooth as her machine usually made them—and in a fifth of the time, too.

She retreated into the living room and plopped into her chair and took out her knitting.

Before she'd gotten very far Geri burst into the house, and what a sight she was! Soaking wet and covered with black mud.

Concerned as much about her home as her daughter, Mrs.

Sanders jumped to her feet to see what was the matter and to prevent Geri from tracking mud into the house. But Geri's eyes were wide with fear and she was panting as if the Devil itself were after her.

"Mick!" she called. "Mick!"

"What is it, Geri?" her mother asked. "Is Mick here?"

"I thought he was with you."

"He was. He hurt his finger on a hook and went to get it cleaned up."

Mrs. Sanders looked aghast at her daughter. She also involuntarily put her hand to her nose. The odor of that mud was overwhelming, as if her daughter had floundered around in dead fish for an hour or two.

"What happened to you?"

"I fell in the lagoon trying to pull in a fish."

That may have been true, but Mrs. Sanders could see from the distraught look in Geri's eyes that there was more to it than that.

"Geri? Is something wrong?"

Geri took a deep breath, shuddered, and seemed to compose herself. "No, honest. I was just thinking about the fish that got away. What a beauty!"

Mrs. Sanders didn't buy it, but knew it was useless to pump Geri till the girl was ready to talk. Meanwhile, she was muddying and stinking up the house.

"Well, you march right upstairs and shower off that mud and filth. You smell awful. Lord only knows what those tourists dump in that water these days."

Geri was just as eager as her mother to get out of the muddy dress and wash off the filth. She trotted upstairs and peeled out of the dress, which clung to her clammily. It fell on the bathroom floor with a plop, and she stepped into the tub, longing to feel the warm needles of the shower washing the disgusting slime off her body.

She turned the shower faucets and waited.

There was a hollow gurgle, a sputter, and a cough. But there was no water.

"Oh no," she groaned, turning the faucets to their full position. "Now what?" God, if she'd have to go the rest of the day with this mud on her she'd just about die!

She'd have just about died if she'd looked up at the shower head while fiddling with the faucets, for probing their way through the holes in the outlet were the heads of a dozen plum-colored worms. Slowly they oozed out of the shower head like hamburger issuing out of a meat grinder.

Geri spun the faucets this way and that, unaware that a horde of vicious, hungry worms was inching its way toward the flesh of her shoulders and breasts, preparing to drop into her long red hair, preparing to burrow into her scalp and skin the way they had done to Roger only moments before.

"Mother?" she called, twiddling the faucets back to the Off position, "please hand me my robe? It's on the chair in my room." Geri decided the only thing to do would be to towel herself dry, perhaps using some drinking water or even club soda from the refrigerator if necessary and drive over to Fly Lake for a quick skinny-dip.

She'd turned the faucets off not a moment too soon.

The worms withdrew into the shower head again and retreated back into the pipe to wait for another opportunity....

The sign said, "M. Elliot, D.D.S."

Mick and Alma looking mystified and disappointed, stood on the wooden front porch of the house that doubled as a dentist's office. They thumped on the door for several minutes before acknowledging that no one was home. Mick's expression seemed to make sense. "I was afraid nobody would be in, I guess you can't drill teeth without electricity." The thought of how it had been done before electricity sent a shiver down Mick's spine.

"Next time, I should wait for a big storm before I make an appointment," Alma wisecracked.

Still holding the skull under his shirt, Mick walked around to the side of the house, Alma tripping after him like a puppy. "Where are you going?'

"I really have to check this thing out," Mick said, peering into a window at the side. This was the office.

Mick tested the window, and it slid up easily. He shook his head in amazement. If this were New York City, not only would the window be locked, it would have a gate behind it, a guard dog behind that, and an hysterical occupant with a police whistle behind that.

Mick boosted himself over the sill and dropped into the office with something less than snakelike smoothness. Alma's entrance wasn't much better; in fact, she fell on top of Mick, knocking the wind out of both of them. They finally got to their feet and looked around the dim, cool room.

There was a marble-topped cabinet on one side of the room, a file cabinet on another, and in the center a fully equipped dentist's chair and stool. "This is really freaky," Alma giggled. Mick went to the filing cabinet and opened several drawers, running his fingers over the labels on the file separators, murmuring the names of patients to himself. "May I ask what you're looking for?" Alma asked.

"Bauter, Baxter, Bayliss, Bean, Beard..." Mick muttered, his fingers tripping excitedly over the file tabs. "Beardsly!"

He opened the file and pulled out a set of X-rays. Holding them up, he tried to match what they revealed to what he'd observed in the skull. "There's three top teeth missing from the skull. I'll need more light."

He went to the window and held the X-rays up again, removing the skull from his shirt and handing it to Alma. She didn't seem gratified to be the recipient of this gift, and reached into her blouse to produce a joint. While holding a human skull, it's never a bad idea to be a little spaced out, she decided.

Mick groaned.

"Anyone I know?" Alma, asked. She put the skull down, lit up, inhaled with a hiss, and joined Mick at the window.

"Shit. Aaron Beardsly."

She looked over his shoulder at the X-ray. No doubt about it. The holes in the upper jaw corresponded exactly to those in the skull. She went back to pick up the skull and they left. Luckily, they'd lingered an extra moment by the window. As they did, a seven-inch worm crawled out of the eye socket of the skull and slithered to the floor.

They returned to the Sanders home double-time, Alma wise-cracking all the way. "I'll bet you could trade Mr. Beardsly's skull for that Nazi bayonet," she said as they rounded the comer and headed for the porch. Mick could hardly believe his ears. Oh, well, what the hell, he said to himself. The kid was young, a little high on grass, and just a bit insensitive.

"Mick! Mick!" It was Geri's voice coming from the house, and it had a ring of urgency and distress. A second later Geri, dressed in shorts and halter, ran out to meet them. Her hair was tangled and damp, and her face was contorted with fright.

"What happened? Where's Roger?" Mick demanded. Geri's eyes widened in a gape as she looked at the skull. An eerie look came over her and she rushed away, sobbing. Mick raced after her, catching her in the kitchen. He grasped her arms in his hands and shook her violently.

She caught her breath and her body drained of tension at last.

"What is it?" Mick asked again, looking steadily into her eyes. "What happened?"

"Mick, it was awful. The worms. They were all over his face. He ran into the woods screaming. There was nothing I could do."

Mick clutched her to his chest tightly, murmuring consolation into her ear. Slowly she pulled herself together.

"I'm really glad you didn't chase after him. If Roger can see, he'll probably try to make his way home too."

Geri ran her trembling hand through her hair. "The worm farm is closer to the lagoon," she acknowledged.

"Then we'll go there and look for him," Mick decided, taking command. Geri nodded weakly.

At that moment, Alma entered the kitchen, holding the skull in cupped hands as if it were a birthday cake. "Aren't you gonna put Mr. Beardsly's skull back in the truck before Roger gets back?" she grinned.

Geri didn't really grasp it at first; then the name sank. in. "Oh, no," she wailed, threatening to go to pieces all over again.

Mick held her tightly again. "Geri!"

But this time there was no controlling her. She grabbed Alma by the shoulders and started shaking her violently. "Don't you even care, you little brat? He was a beautiful old man."

Geri's kid sister whimpered. "Who said I didn't care?"

Mick stepped between them. "Cut it out."

"What's going on down there?" Mrs. Sanders shouted. A moment later she entered the kitchen, to find dead silence. Mick and her daughters were frozen in awkward postures of feigned innocence. "Just what are you fighting about?" Mrs. Sanders demanded.

One thing you could say about Geri and Alma: they fought like cat and dog, but against the common enemy—their mother—they were fiercely loyal to each other.

"Nothing," Alma said sweetly.

"Young lady," Mrs. Sanders started to say angrily. It was hot, Mrs. Sanders was exhausted from the morning's preparations, and her nerves were frayed by the storm and all the inconvenience it had caused. At the moment she felt almost ready to go off the deep end.

"I...told her that it was her turn to serve dinner tonight," Geri said. Lying did not come too facilely to her tongue, but it was the best explanation she could come up with on short notice.

Mrs. Sanders glared at Alma, who'd backed away and deposited the skull on a table behind a short wall separating the kitchen from the back door. "Since Geri has a guest, I think it would be a nice gesture if you offered to serve dinner, whether it's your turn or not."

Alma nodded. "It's settled," Mrs. Sanders said sternly. She looked at Geri. "Did you tell Alma that you invited Roger for dinner?"

Geri gulped. "No, I forgot."

"Alma, let's try to think of an extra side dish," Mrs. Sanders touched the collar of her blouse and looked dreamily off into space. "Lord only knows when's the last time we had two hungry men around here," she murmured coyly, and then left.

The two girls heaved a great gust of relief. "I'm sorry," Geri said, offering a conciliatory hand to Alma.

Alma accepted it. The sisters squabbled all the time, but like squalls their fights passed quickly enough. "It's all right," said Alma. "I'm really worried about her. I've never seen her this freaked out."

"Try to stay with her till we get back, okay?" Geri said.

Alma nodded.

Mick and Geri left the house. Alma decided it would be a good idea to deposit the skull in a less visible place. She picked it up and gazed at it. Suddenly, for the first time, the enormity of it struck her: just a few days ago, this bad been a human being and one she'd known well since childhood. She clapped her hand over her mouth and ran into the backyard gagging.

Chapter Eleven

"I wonder what made those worms act that way?" Mick pondered aloud as they got into the car. "You think maybe Roger's old man is fooling around with electricity?"

"What electricity?" Geri asked.

"Good point!' said Mick, his aspirations to become a Sherlock Holmes gravely checked. What electricity indeed? There wasn't so much as a volt of the stuff to be found anywhere in Fly Creek outside of automobile batteries.

They drove a short way down the back road of the Grimes' property in the hopes of seeing Mr. Grimes or his son. There was no sign of either, just acres and acres of rich, newly tilled soil, the breeding ground for worms too numerous to count.

They arrived at a shack that stood at the end of the farm opposite the Grimes' home, a crude, unpainted structure of warped gray siding and rotten shingles. It was surrounded by crates and crate boards, rusting implements, and the detritus of some twenty years of labor without adequate help to keep the place trim.

The sky overhead had begun to cloud as it habitually did late in the afternoon here on the shores of the Atlantic Ocean. The sun had sunk behind some of these clouds, throwing ominous shafts of shadowless pearly light over the deserted aspect of the farm. The birds had begun to cease their relentless twitter, and a breeze had gotten up, swaying the trees on the perimeter of the farm like troupes of lugubrious dancers.

Geri, still deeply shaken by her recent traumatic experience in the rowboat with Roger, put her hand on the door handle but med almost paralytically incapable of getting out.

Mick appreciated this and told her to wait in the car. "I hope we find him before it gets dark," he said, getting out. This was not strictly true. From Geri's description of the dreadful damage inflicted on Roger's face, Mick wasn't sure he'd want to confront him face *to* face in this fading light. Young and healthy though he was, there was no law saying he couldn't have a heart attack if the fright were intense enough. His memory of that worm burrowing under his finger was fresh enough—he had the pain of the wound to remind him, if nothing else—to conjure the most gruesome fantasy of what a man's face would look like if it took the attack of a dozen *of* the crazed creatures at one time.

But the most gruesome fantasy he could conjure up was no match for the real thing.

Had he turned around he'd have seen it.

Had Geri turned around she'd have seen it too, for it had staggered out of the woods behind the cat and stood, wavering like a scarecrow m the wind, about twenty yards away. "Thing" was the right word for it, too, for this could truly not be called a human being. Where a face had been were now a dozen burrows, each as wide as the entry hole of a .38 caliber slug, and from out of each the tail of a worm flicked and quivered. The cheeks were furrowed where the worms had insinuated then: way under the flesh. Dried blood and gore blotched his face. His eyes stared lifelessly out of a mutilated head.

His hands hung limply at his side. Apparently, some of the worms had penetrated the cavities of his skull and entered the brain, and a few had probably damaged his brain sufficiently to sever some of the host's motor centers. Thus, he'd lost either his will to resist and fight off the parasites under his flesh, or his ability, or both.

But they hadn't penetrated all of his brain. There was enough left to determine to destroy the humans who had inflicted this living death upon him.

He began advancing on the car. If Geri had looked in the rear-view mirror she'd have seen it, but she sat slumped down in the driver's seat, trying to subdue the attack of nerves that had left her limp in the wake of the afternoon's events.

Roger staggered to within a few yards of the car. With lifeless eyes he watched Mick poking around the shack. Then he stopped.

Mick had picked up a spade.

In the dim reaches of Roger's tortured brain he saw the spade as a possible weapon to be used against him if he attacked Geri now. Faltering, he studied the hated intruder, weighing strength against strength, and concluded the odds were too high. This was not the right time. Wavering, the tortured boy turned and staggered off into the woods again, to bride his time.

Mick and Geri never knew how close they'd come.

But they would, soon enough.

Mick probed the fresh soil around the shack with the spade. He'd found a fragment of yellow plaid cloth near one of the crates and remembered that Mr. Grimes had been wearing a shirt of that same color earlier in the day. Poking in the soil, he came across a few splintered fragments of crate material, and they seemed fresh and dry. He looked around some more and then stopped dead in his tracks. A little crimson patch on a plot of grass. And trailing away from it, dried crimson dots about a foot apart. Blood.

The trail led to an area behind a stack of crates and a low growth of weeds. Hesitantly Mick followed the trail, knowing he would find something he didn't want to see, yet drawn to it compellingly. He didn't know why; he simply knew he could not turn his back on whatever it was that lay behind those crates.

Grasping the handle of the spade tightly, preparing to swing with all his might at whatever enemy might lurk behind that stack of boxes, he stepped cautiously along the trail of blood and peered around the side of the crates.

Mick's eyes shut tightly, and a wince escaped his lips involuntarily.

It was Willie Grimes, dead.

He lay on his back, his mud-spattered face contorted in a ghastly grimace, proclaiming a pain that no human should be asked to endure. His eyes stared up at the sky, the life mercifully drained from them.

There was no indication of what had killed the poor man. Mick kneeled down to examine the chest for wounds and was about to reach out to unbutton the man's shirt when he thought he saw Grimes's chest rise and fall. Could it be that he was alive?

Mick grabbed the shirt with both hands and tore it open at the buttons in order to put his ear to Grimes's chest and listen for a heartbeat.

What Mick saw in place of a chest was a sight that he could carry in his mind's eye for the rest of his life.

They had eaten away the flesh of his chest and abdomen and were feasting on his entrails. There must have been a thousand of them, a sea of worms writhing in his heart, stomach, liver, intestines, kidneys. The man's body was virtually alive with worms, methodically eating their way through him until his bones would be as clean those of Mr. Beardsly.

It was too much for Mick. His circuits overloaded. It had started with the arduous, hot bus ride, the trek through the mosquito-infested wood, the humiliating fall into the mudhole, the insults suffered at the hands of the sheriff, the worm in his glass, the skeleton in Beardsly's yard, the vicious worm-bite in the boat. Was any man capable of enduring so many blows without striking out at the malevolent providence that had inflicted them on him? No. No, this was too much.

He grasped the spade and swung it down with all his might on the writhing mass of worm-infested guts. *SPLAT!* Blood and slime spattered in every direction. Again: *SPLAT!* He heard himself cursing as he struck the seething body of Willie Grimes again and again.

SPLAT! SPLAT! SPLAT! SPLAT!

Weeping openly, Mick threw down the shovel and staggered away, his rage spent, his fury drained. Nearing the car, he pulled himself together. Geri had gone through hell herself and he needed to be strong for her. He took a deep breath, wiped the tears off his cheeks, and checked the speed of his flight, bringing it down to a calm and confident stride.

"Did you see him?" Geri asked apprehensively.

"Get back in the car," he ordered in a controlled voice, getting in. "Give me the key."

"I left it in the ignition," Geri said, sliding over into the passenger's seat.

Mick started the car and spun rubber in the soft soil before the rear tires finally caught on the dirt road. The car leaped forward and hurtled down the road as if the Devil itself were in pursuit, which in a sense was the truth. They came across the main road and Mick swerved onto it with a squeal of tires.

"Will this road get me back to town?"

"Just keep going straight," Geri said, looking at him quizzically. She studied his face. Lines of tension drew his mouth tight, and the veins stood out on his neck as if he was fighting to hold back a scream. "What did you see?" Geri asked the question with more fear than curiosity: she was not at all sure she wanted to hear the answer.

Mick's sense of humor returned for a moment. "Talk about New York! Two corpses in one day! Next time, *you* come and visit *me.*"

"Roger?" she asked, gritting her teeth for the devastating reply.

Mick's reply was not the one she'd been expecting, but it was devastating, nevertheless.

"No, his father."

Though he didn't know the road, Mick prove recklessly, hitting eighty miles an hour at one point. Geri was almost too numb to be scared—almost, but not completely. She sucked in her breath and pumped the floor in front of the passenger's seat as if there were a brake pedal down there. She wished there had been. There'd been enough deaths around here without adding two more.

She looked at Mick and somehow sensed that he was heading for town in order to seek Sheriff Reston. That was a very gutsy thing to do, considering how badly he had fared with him in the last two encounters, and what the sheriff had said to him on the second of these. Yet it had to be done; he had to convince the man that he wasn't simply some wise-ass from New York City come here to have fun at the expense of the country bumpkins; had to convince him it was a matter of life or death.

Geri's intuition proved correct. The station wagon flew past the Town Limits sign—speed 30 MPH—and skidded to a halt in front of the old brick courthouse, where the sheriff's office was.

Their heels made hollow *click-clacks* on the marble floor as they entered and rushed down the corridor where the office was located. An elderly lady was mopping the corridor floor.

"Is Sheriff Reston here?" Mick asked, breathlessly. "Well, he was," the lady drawled.

She continued mopping, oblivious to the urgency of their mission. At length she looked up. "Why, Geraldine. What are you doing here?"

"Hi, Mrs. Norton," Geri said, glancing at Mick. Geri hated her name and anyone who used it. She'd been Geri since the age of five, but there were still a few fuds who insisted on calling her Geraldine.

"Did your mother get the yarn I sent her?" She turned to Mick and started talking to him as if they'd been friends for twenty years. "I'm allergic to wool, but I love to knit. I use that orlon, you know."

Mick nodded impatiently, hoping to get a word in edgewise or any other wise. Wool! Orlon! The world was being invaded by man-eating worms and this, this...

"She promised me," the cleaning woman went on, "she'd knit me a shawl. Not for me—for my daughter. It's a surprise."

Mick sighed impatiently. "Is he around?" "Who?"

"Sheriff Reston," Geri said with a sharp edge to her voice.

"Oh. yes. I mean, no, he's not here. He might be having his dinner now. I couldn't tell you what time it is 'cause all the clocks stopped."

"It's really important that we talk to him." Geri stressed, bending over backward to be nice to a woman she cheerfully would have liked to throttle.

"Oh, well, you might find him over at the Casa Roma," she said, finally.

The two young people darted out of the courthouse. The cleaning lady shrugged and went back to her mopping. What, she wondered, could be so all-fired important they couldn't stand around and shoot the breeze with an old lady for a few minutes. Children these days—really!

There is a Casa Roma in every small town, not always known by that name but known by the pathetic mural of Rome (or Naples or Venice) done by some talentless local artist, usually the wife of the owner, and the tattered gingham tablecloths and the chianti bottles laden with colorful wax drippings and sputtering candle and the pimply-faced waiters and waitresses looking dumb in their gypsy costumes.

Actually, Fly Creek's Casa Roma looked halfway attractive at this hour—dusk—because all the candles had been lit to compensate for the loss of electricity, and the place had a romantic glow that made even Sheriff Reston's sneering face look rather benign.

He even smiled at Geri when she and Mick approached his table, and when he saw Mick he merely turned the corners of his mouth down, indicating no more irritation than if the town drunk had raised his voice at the bar.

The reason for the sheriff's tolerant attitude quickly became apparent. His dinner companion was the same woman who'd accompanied him to lunch, the tall, dark-haired woman in white with the lost, confused expression on her face. Sheriff Reston was not about to display an ill-temper in front of a woman he was trying to impress, a woman he hoped would be his companion for breakfast tomorrow morning, and everything between these two meals as well.

"Sheriff Reston," Geri said, stepping in front of Mick. She knew how sparks flew between the two men, and she wanted to avoid that kind of trouble when there was trouble of a much more serious kind brewing outside the town. "Please excuse us, but it's very important."

He broke a roll, smeared some butter on it, and chewed on it, looking at Geri indifferently.

Mick had hoped Geri would be able to pin down Reston's attention, but apparently she'd failed. He drew her aside and looked at the sheriff. "I know you think I'm a troublemaker," he said.

"Now that's the first thing you've said that I can buy," the sheriff laughed. He smiled cockily at his dinner companion, then frowned as he remembered the antique necklace around her neck. Mick and Geri noticed it too and suppressed a laugh. Geri and her mother had sold it to him just a few hours earlier —for his "wife". Reston looked terribly discomfited.

Fortunately, the matter was dropped as the waitress came to the table straining under a platter of food. She laid it on a serving table, removed the tops off two stainless steel plates, and set the plates in front of Reston and the woman. The plates were piled high with—spaghetti.

Under normal circumstances, Mick and Geri wouldn't have blanched at the sight of these long tubes of pasta, tangled in a great knotty mass and covered with a blood-colored sauce. Indeed, considering that this was, after all, an Italian restaurant, they'd have been surprised if anything else were served here.

But these were not normal circumstances, and at the sight of this spaghetti their knees went weak, and they turned pale.

They averted their eyes for a moment, took charge of themselves, and faced the sheriff again. "I don't know how to go about this, Sheriff," Mick said boldly, "but I have proof that the skeleton we found was the remains of Aaron Beardsly."

In his line of work, Sheriff Reston came across a lot of folks who fancied themselves private eyes. He could n w add this city punk to the list. "That so?" he said patronizingly, tucking his napkin into the neck of his shirt. He picked up his fork and a spoon and began twirling long strands of the spaghetti into an orderly braid around the fork. "What kind of proof?"

Mick watched the spaghetti-wrapping hypnotically, trying hard to keep from gagging. With all he'd done to the sheriff in the last eight or ten hours, he couldn't imagine I the man appreciating it if Mick threw up on his dinner.

"We found another body," Mick announced. "It was Mr. Grimes."

The sheriff's hand paused an instant as it conveyed his first forkful of spaghetti to his open mouth, but that was his only reaction to the news. He blinked, then bit into the spaghetti. Several strings of it hung out of his lips, dangling like blood-colored-worms. He sucked at these and they wriggled around his chin.

"Tell him about the worms," Geri prompted behind Mick.

It was plain to see that the sheriff and his friend did not appreciate a reference to worms as they were wrapping their lips around their dinner. Reston sucked at the two or three strands that dangled from his lips, and they slithered into his mouth at last. Geri stared. She actually swayed on her feet at the sight. She could not help but think of poor Roger as the invading worms, tails wriggling like these spaghetti ends, burrowed their way into his face.

"Worms?" asked Sheriff Reston, eyebrows raised.

"They bite," Geri said quickly, following up on the sheriff's first sign of interest. "It's horrible. Thousands of them. They attacked Roger Grimes and we still can't find him."

The sheriff's companion had raised a forkful of spaghetti to her sensuous open lips, but now she wrinkled her nose, stared at the food, and placed the fork back on her plate.

This time the sheriff didn't hesitate. He shoveled a load of spaghetti into his maw and ground it resoundingly, lips smacking, sauce dribbling over his lower lip. But his friend was obviously revolted, and he didn't care much for that.

"If you'll only come with us to the worm farm, I can prove it to you," Mick pleaded.

The sheriff's companion had turned pale and looked at his pleadingly, asking him with her deep dark eyes whether there weren't some way he could stop this disgusting conversation before it ruined her meal entirely. That did it. Up to now the sheriff had been patient with these two. Especially with Geri. He could understand the city kid pulling a bit like this, but he'd never have expected it from a nice girl like Geri. The time had come to put a stop to it.

From under his blond eyebrows, he cast his deadly gaze at Mick, "Fella, there's a lot of spaghetti here. Might take us ten, fifteen minutes to finish it. That's a bigger head start than you deserve."

He delivered his threat with such finality that Mick couldn't believe it when Geri started to remonstrate with him. "But Mr. Reston..."

"Geri," Mick commanded, restraining her by the arm. "Let's go."

Chapter Twelve

One thing that these teenagers could say in favor of the blackout, reflected Mr. Quigley as he polished some glass beer steins behind his bar: it made it easier for them to do their illegal drinking. With only candlelight to see by, they were bold enough to put their booze right up on the table, challenging him to say something about it. He supposed he should, but what the hell, the kids weren't hurting anybody, nor were they overdoing it with the liquor. Of course, if Sheriff Reston came in, that flask had better disappear pronto or he'd lose his license. Well, maybe not, Sheriff Reston was pretty tolerant about these things, especially when his tolerance was stimulated by a twenty dollar bill passed into his hand when he shook it.

The teenagers, Jeff, Eddie, and Susanne, were fooling around with the bayonet Eddie had brought to sell or swap with Geri's city boyfriend. Jeff held it close to the candle, studying the workmanship and the German engraving that proved the weapon was authentic. Suddenly Jeff thrust the knife out at his pal, grazing the startled kid's gizzard.

"Hey, watch out where you point that thing," Eddie warned. He didn't find such pranks funny—unless he was on the handle end of them and Jeff was on the blade end.

They took another swig of the flask, washed it down with Coke, and stared through the window of the bar, hoping to make out through the darkness the person they'd come here to meet. "I'll bet you that guy doesn't even show up," Eddie said despairingly, his hopes of turning a few bucks on this piece of junk fading like the light of his guttering candle.

"There they are!" Susanne squealed, tapping on the window to get Mick's attention.

Mick and Geri acknowledged them and a moment later entered the bar.

"Here she is," Eddie said, proudly displaying the bayonet. It gleamed a glorious yellow in the reflected glow of the candle.

Mick took it and held it respectfully, left palm supporting the haft, right palm the steel blade He examined it closely, though truth to tell, his heart wasn't in it right now, with far more important matters weighing on his mind. The blade was beautifully honed on both cutting edges, and Mick tested the sharpness on the hair of his forearm. Several hairs floated down to the tabletop, testifying to the keenness of the blade. Mick then hefted the bayonet, balancing it on his index finger. You had to hand it to the Nazis: they sure did make excellent instruments of war.

Susanne found weapons boring and peered out the window, trying to see who was with whom on the town's main street, though she had only pale blue starlight to aid her vision. But there is no eye so sharp as that of a gossip, and her straining surveillance was rewarded by the sight of a couple leaving the Casa Roma and strolling toward the courthouse.

"Hey, dig it, there's your answer," she said lustily.

"Answer to what?" one of the boys asked.

"Where he's gonna take her."

The kids crowded against the window and followed Sheriff Reston and the woman in white with excited eyes. Yes, they were definitely going up the courthouse steps. Reston fumbled with a chain heavy with keys until he found the right one, then unlocked the door. With a glance behind him, he ushered the woman in, then slipped in behind her, hastily shutting the courthouse door and locking it behind him. The kids peered across the street, hoping to see something more, but had to settle for the faint glitter of a candle as Reston escorted the woman to the second floor of the courthouse.

"I wonder what he's up to," Eddie mused "There aren't any beds in there."

Jeff and Susanne giggled. They knew that as far as the lecherous Sheriff Reston was concerned, where there was a will there would be a way. Somewhere in that building was a bed, you could count on it as surely as you could depend on daybreak.

Mick and Geri did not participate in this little spry episode. They were too distracted by what they had seen, and too distressed by what they feared was to come. Mick looked at the blade of the bayonet as if it were a crystal ball that could help him solve the mystery of the agitated worms. He was thinking about Mr. Beardsly's skeleton. What had killed the man? Natural causes? Or murder? And how had his bones been transported from the yard of his home to the back of the Grimes' truck? Was there any connection between this and the uprising of the worms?

Mick vowed that once this thing was over, he'd leave detective work to the professionals. But right now he was sorely vexed and desperate to get some insight into the Beardsly case. "What time did you talk to Beardsly on the phone?" he asked Geri quietly, so that Alma's friends couldn't hear.

"I don't know," Geri said, scratching the back of her head. "Not too late." She closed her eyes and made an effort to remember. It came to her. "Oh, just before the lights went out. There was this big flash of lightning and thunder. All the lights went out. He said he had to get some candles so he couldn't talk any more. The phones went dead before I could say goodbye."

"Well," said a voice, penetrating through the fog of Mick's reflections. "What do you think?"

Mick blinked and returned to the here and now of Quigley's Bar. Eddie was leaning over his shoulder, gesturing at the bayonet. Mick looked at him. "Very nice."

"Tell you what," the kid said. "Since you're a friend of Geri's and all, twenty bucks and she's yours."

Mick looked him straight in the eye. "No, for twenty bucks she's *yours.*" Abruptly he got to his feet and was out of the bar, Geri tagging behind, before Eddie could lower his price. Eddie shook his head, wondering about these New York City types. It was true that an effective bargaining ploy, when a potential buyer thought the price of an item too high, was to walk away. But this guy Mick was walking too far too fast. That looked like No Sale. Oh well, there were lots of other suckers in the world, he said to himself, tossing down the contents of his flask....

"Where we going?" Geri asked, walking double-time after Mick.

"Back to Beardsly's," he said as they arrived at the car.

This announcement pleased Geri very little. Wandering around the sites of recent deaths where bodies had been consumed by vicious worms was not precisely what she'd expected to do with Mick when she'd invited him down to Fly Creek.

Beardsly's house, silhouetted against the starry sky, virtually shrieked warnings at them to call off their investigation. The night sounds of crickets and toads and bullfrogs reverberated through the black woods, but they listened for another sound even though they had no idea what that sound would be like: the sound of worms. As Geri trod the ground of the Beardsly property, she wondered if her next step would fall on a seething mass of them, which would swarm over her feet and slither up her legs, gnawing her flesh as they went along, burrowing under it, eating their way up her calves, knees, and thighs until....

She shook her head, trying to shake off the hideous fantasies that had crawled out of her imagination. She stayed very close to Mick as he led her to the edge of the woods where they had first come across the bones. "What do you expect to find?" she said.

They stood over the patch of ground, mutely taking in the vibrations of the awful event that had taken place here scarcely more than twenty-four hours earlier. Mick looked back at the house's antique shop. "What was he doing in the shop that late at night?"

She shrugged. "He fiddles—uh, fiddled—with the antiques, gluing and painting things."

Mick walked across the yard in back of the shop. Looking down as he did, he circled his way around to the other side of the shop, Geri trailing behind, mystified. Suddenly Mick stopped and stooped over what appeared to be a fragment of a soaked, paint-stained smock, torn almost in half.

He looked over his shoulder, gauging the distance between this point and the place where they'd discovered the skeleton. Then he looked at the shed at the side of the shop.

"What's in there?"

"Tools, paint, brushes, like that I think he gets his well water from in there."

"Candles?"

Geri held her palms up, indicating she didn't really know. Could be.

Mick approached the shed, stood before it for a moment, listening. Then he put his shoulder to the door and his hand on the handle. Geri backed away and Mick hesitated. What was he looking for? What did he hope to find? What if the shed were filled with…?

Mick decided that whatever was on the other side of that door was a mystery best not solved for now. He walked away, grasping Geri tightly by the arm and guiding her firmly to the car.

"I have a feeling Roger and his father are off the hook as far as killing Beardsly is concerned."

As they climbed into the car, Mick taking the wheel, he elaborated. "I think Roger followed us here, spying on us like a little kid. Then he saw the..." It still didn't make sense. "But why take the skeleton?"

It did make sense to Geri. She remembered that just before Roger had made that fatal pass at her in the rowboat, he had said something about having a surprise for her. "That was the surprise," she explained.

Mick turned into the road and looked at Geri, hungering for the answer.

"He wanted to surprise me with the skeleton. It could bring at least a hundred dollars at one of the shows. Roger was talking about going into business with me just before..."

Yes, that was it. It had been Roger who'd picked up the skeleton and loaded it on the truck. *After* someone—or something—had killed Mr. Beardsly. That was the last piece of the puzzle. She looked at Mick, hoping he could fit it in. "Then who...?"

He could. "The worms."

Chapter Thirteen

The table was set magnificently. Mrs. Sanders had set out her best antique linen tablecloth with the embroidered border and matching napkins, the best china and glassware, and an English silver service that had been in the family for as long as anyone could remember. She'd even gone into the garden and cut fresh flowers for the centerpiece. The only thing that was out of place was Roger. He was very late, and after waiting as long as was decent, she'd yielded to Geri's suggestion that they begin without him.

The sight of that empty fifth place at the table had thrown her even deeper into the depression that had come over her in the kitchen, the kind of depression that had come over her with more and more frequency since her husband's death. She had hoped that the presence of two attractive males at the dinner table, seated beside two young and wholesome girls, would ring a little laughter and happiness into her increasingly dark and humorless life. But now that empty chair at the table was like a grin with one tooth prominently missing. She could think only of the man missing from her life, the man molding in his grave. She gazed with nearly lifeless eyes at the splendid spread laid out on the table.

No, she mustn't go on this way, she told herself. That way lay misery and death. She must try to keep out of it, to involve herself in life, to remain young by cultivating the young. She would make an effort.

Turning to Mick, she said, "How do you like Fly Creek?" It was pretty feeble, admittedly, but it was a start.

"Oh, fine," Mick said. "It's nice to get away from the city." There was something insincere in the way he said it, as if his mind had removed itself to wander elsewhere while his lips mouthed meaningless replies to meaningless questions. The boy had been behaving quite peculiarly ever since he and Geri had returned home a little while ago. What was distracting him? Mrs. Sanders wondered. Probably just in love with Geri, that's all.

But would being in love account for that strange, haunted look in his eyes, as if something unspeakably savage were dogging his footsteps?

Most puzzling....

Geri and Alma huddled at the sideboard, cutting the roast and putting the finishing touches on the side dishes. They kept up a pleasant demeanor, so as not to alarm their mother, but their voices gave away the real state of their emotions. "Attacked!" Alma whispered.

Geri shrank and signaled with her hand for Alma to cool it and keep her voice down. Then she put her face close to Alma's and spoke almost inaudibly. "We're not sure. Mick thinks Mr. Beardsly went to his shed to get candles when the lights went out. He still had the match book when we found him."

"Did you look in the shed?" Alma asked, laying a sprig of parsley across the sweet potatoes.

"No," Geri said, her memory drawing her back to that fateful moment when Mick had actually stood with his shoulder against the shed door, and then decided not to satisfy his curiosity. "I'm glad we didn't," she said.

They picked up the platters and casserole dishes and carried them to the table.

Mrs. Sanders looked absolutely desolate. "Did you try Roger next door? I feel terrible starting without him."

Geri and Mick exchanged glances, and Mick actually came close to breaking into an ironic smile. Geri interpreted it to mean, "You wouldn't feel so terrible starting without him if you knew what we know."

"He's probably working late at the farm," Geri said as nonchalantly as possible.

Mrs. Sanders clucked and shook her head. "Willie doesn't appreciate how hard that poor boy works. I never could understand that man."

Geri and Alma took their seats. Geri placed herself with Alma on one side and her mother on the other.

"That's Roger's seat, dear," said Mrs. Sanders. "What's the difference?"

"I thought you'd want to sit next to Mick," she said sadly. Then she sighed lugubriously. "I guess it doesn't make a difference, does it?"

It didn't as far as Geri was concerned, but she did want to please her mother, who seemed these days to be hunting for reasons to be unhappy. Geri got up and sat down again beside Mick.

The family started passing the food around, and though the meal could have been festive, a celebration of their conquest over the electricity failure, a romantic evening of candlelit gaiety, it was closer to a wake than anything else. Nothing was heard but the hollow tinkle of silver on china, chewing sounds, and an occasional "Pass the salt" or "May I have some more cranberries?"

Oh yes, there was one other sound. The first time they'd heard it they'd paused in their eating to cock their ears and look at each other curiously. It was a splintery cracking sound, as if someone outside were bending a green branch over his knee.

Only it was louder than that. Much louder indeed, as if someone were bending an entire adult tree over his knee. Geri had gotten up and looked out the window into the blackness of the night, but she saw nothing, nothing but the enormous old elm tree that had stood like a friendly sentinel, casting its leafy protection over their home, ever since the house had been built.

Geri shrugged and returned to the dinner table, but from that point on she listened for the sound again. She wondered if Roger was out there, lurking, his tortured body driving him to seek help among the only people who cared about him.

The second *CR-A-A-A-CK* was disconcertingly loud, causing Mick to leap to his feet, heart pounding madly in his chest. He too had thought of Roger. but when he went to the window he saw nothing but the old elm tree, its tall branches swaying in the stiff breeze that had got up a while ago and was now whistling through the surrounding woods.

Mick returned to the table but didn't continue eating. He thought about that sound, and the tree...*the tree!* Of course! Last night's storm had probably dislodged the elm tree's secure hold in the ground. All day that tree's roots had bathed in the muddy soil of the storm's inundation, grappling for solidity the way a drowning person reaches for a spar or life preserver to clutch before going under. And there may have been another element, too: worms.

My God! Mick's mind shrieked at him. The worms! If light was their enemy, then the nighttime, if the moon and stars were obscured by a cloud layer as they were tonight, would bring them to the surface of the earth in a frenzy of activity, the way they'd done with Mr. Beardsly and Willie Grimes. Especially if they were being stimulated by some force, as they seemed to be. That was the one aspect of this mystery that didn't yet jibe in Mick's mind: what was making the worms so desperately hungry?

Whatever it was, with the darkness would come the boiling ferment of millions of starving worms. Their turmoil would weaken the soil beneath any tree whose roots had been dislodged by the storm.

And if a stiff breeze were to begin whipping through the branches of such a tree...

Mick's mind had computed all this in less than a second or two, but even while the frightened conclusion was laboring to be born his muscles had already reacted. He leaped to his feet, grasping Geri and Mrs. Sanders each by an arm, and hauled them to their feet hoping to get them and Alma the hell out of there before...

But it was too late. This time the cracking sound was accompanied by a rustling of leaves as if a giant had encircled the tree trunk in his arms and was bringing the tree around like an ax to score a fatal blow against the house.

A deafening crash filled the air. Plaster sprayed the table with flakes and dust and an instant later the ceiling collapsed, sending splintered wood darting in all directions. Only by dint of his quick thinking had Mick saved the lives of Geri and her mother, for the trunk landed with a thud in the place where their chairs had been an instant before.

For a moment there was deadly silence. Then Alma burst into sobs.

Mick had been knocked off his feet by the impact, and his knees felt bruised where he'd fallen on them, but aside from that he didn't seem the worse for having a tree fall on him. Alma was sobbing but it sounded like they were sobs of fright rather than of pain.

Mrs. Sanders lay on the floor, her body bridged but fortunately not touched by a bowed branch. She stared up at the night sky pouring in through what was left of the roof and seemed indifferent to the tragedy which had befallen the house and which had nearly befallen her and her family. Her indifference, in fact, was frightening. She seemed to have disassociated herself entirely from the world. Geri kneeled over her, murmuring words of comfort. Her mother acknowledged them with a lifeless smile.

Mick looked over at them. "It's all right," Geri said. "Nobody's hurt."

Relieved, Mick took a deep draught of air into his lungs, dusted himself off, and picked his way through the debris, following the shattered tree trunk to its base outside the house. Yes, it had been just as he'd thought. The soft soil and strong winds had combined to loosen the grip of the roots in the earth until at last the ancient elm had given up the ghost and fallen.

At the foot of the tree, Mick could see silhouetted in the blue-black backdrop of the starry sky the root ball of the tree, an enormous knot of roots and soil measuring seven or eight feet in diameter. He cocked his ears and listened.

It was indistinct at first. then it became sharper and louder: a turbulent sound like laundry sloshing around in a washing machine, only much more ominous. He touched his hand to the tree trunk and felt it vibrating, as if something living was gnawing its way into the heart of the wood.

Cautiously he made his way down the trunk, to the root ball for a look at what was causing that vibration.

The sight all but took his breath away.

"Geri? Could you come out here a second?" he said, struggling to maintain a calm voice.

Geri took Alma's arm and led her to their mother, who'd slid out from under the branch and was now sitting on it, shaking violently, trembling fingers raking her hair and face. Alma had gotten hold of herself and offered what aid she could to a woman who seemed to be heading around the bend with mounting speed. "Stay with her, Alma," Geri said.

But it wasn't that easy to tum Mrs. Sanders over to Alma. The poor woman clutched Geri's arm as if Geri were abandoning her to a pitful of fiends. Patiently, Geri pried her mother's hand away, keeping up a line of comforting chatter. "I'm just going outside. I'll be right back."

At length Alma took over the ministrations and Geri slipped away, climbing over the legs of the table that jutted into the air like those of a dead horse frozen in an ice storm. It was quite dark outside except for a tinge of blush in the western sky where the sun's last influence could be seen. Geri called Mick's name and was answered by a quivering voice and noticed a shadow beside the root ball, which stood on its side like an immense coin lying on its side.

She joined Mick, who stood gaping at the root ball with eyes transfixed. She turned to see what had provoked the fascination.

Her knees almost gave out.

A scream rose unbidden to her throat. Anticipating this, Mick clapped his band over her mouth. All they needed, after the collapse of the tree on their house, was this new threat, and they'd have to have Mrs. Sanders permanently committed to an insane asylum.

"Geri," Mick pleaded, trying to hold the situation together, "listen to me. Is there any gasoline around?"

Geri breathed deeply several times before she could trust herself to answer without bursting into a hysterical shriek. "In… in the storage room under the back porch."

Mick put both hands on her shoulders. Through the darkness she could see and feel the comforting warmth of his solicitude, and she thanked the very stars above that she had him during this ordeal. Lord only knew what she'd have done without his quiet strength and engaging sense of humor. "Hey, are you all right?" he asked, drawing her to him.

She nodded bravely, then released him.

He moved fast picking his way through fragments of shattered limbs, lathing, and shingles to the back porch. In the long minute that be was gone, Geri forced herself to look upon the root ball of the old elm tree.

It was alive with crawling worms. They seethed like noodles in a cauldron, their hooded faces probing the sky, their pincer jaws snapping at the air in the hopes of capturing any morsel that might be unfortunate enough to alight on them.

Geri, nauseated to the bottom of her stomach, nevertheless couldn't pull her eyes away, and even found herself drawn to the sight, lured by the seduction of horror the way people are attracted by the scenes of airplane accidents or mass-murder gravesites. She even managed a rather bizarre mental association as she wondered how many worms there were in this living mass of slimy flesh. If there were approximately two dozen worms in the box in the rowboat today—the box was about six inches high, four wide, and three deep, or 7 cubic inches, how many would there by in a circular space 84 inches in diameter or so, when the worms were perhaps six inches deep? Let's see, if she remembered her math correctly, C equals pi times the diameter. But C is the circumference, right? And what does that have to do with 24 worms in a space of 72 cubic inches?

"God, there must be tens of thousands of them," Mick gasped, rescuing her from the necessity of further calculation.

He opened the can of gasoline and tilted it over the root ball The worms reacted angrily to the chemical substances, doubling the rate at which they entwined with each other like some elaborate ballet choreographed by a maniac.

Mick reached into his pocket for the trusty lighter that had helped him out of more than one tricky situation today. In the orange flame-glow the turmoil redoubled as the worms fought with one another for a retreat from the abhorrent light. As Mick brought his hand closer the worms radiated away from it like a mass of rioters fleeing a teargas grenade dropped in their midst.

All at once, with a whoosh, the root ball exploded in a mushroom of flame. The heat threw Mick and Geri back a yard, then they grasped hands and watched mutely as the writhing mass seemed to melt before their eyes, filling the air with an acrid odor of roasting worm-flesh that exceeded rotting vegetables or putrefying flesh by a factor of thousands.

For a moment the flames started to travel up the fallen tree trunk toward the house and Mick could have kicked himself for not having taken a precaution against this happening, but after crawling a foot or two, the orange flames retreated and shrank. "I don't think the tree will catch. It's too wet. Get ready to throw dirt into it to put out the flames."

They kneeled on the earth and started to scratch up some topsoil to throw on the conflagration, but both of them jumped away simultaneously as they realized that just below the surface, armies of worms seethed, ready to take the place of those that had just perished.

Luckily the flames, after consuming the fleshy fuel of worms, encountered the dampness of the tree trunk itself and began to die out. After stomping on a little circle of fugitive fire that had spread out about a yard from the root ball, Mick watched in dumb fascination at another new phenomenon.

"What is it?" Geri asked, trying to read his face.

Mick looked down at the ground, and Geri sucked her breath in sharply. In the same spot where their scratching had revealed a virtual sea of worms, now there was nothing, nothing but muddy earth.

"Mick, why is this happening?" Geri whimpered.

"Something is making them go crazy, driving them out of the ground," Mick said, as much to himself as to her. He stared at the ground as if it were a book to be read if the scholar could only penetrate the obscurity of the language. Mick felt very close to the secret, if only… if only….

Wait a minute. Something was trying to filter into his awareness. Something Roger had told them about his father's experiments with worms. One experiment in particular, which had been the cause of the accident that left Roger without the top half of a thumb. An experiment involving...

"ELECTRICITY!" Mick shouted.

Geri looked at him uncertainly. "But...there isn't any."

"Yes there is!" he said with mounting excitement. "The

power lines that went down are still sending juice into the ground. Millions of watts and soaking wet mud to act as a conductor!"

They looked at the hole where they'd seen worms beyond reckoning moments before.

"As soon as the light hits them, they disappear," Mick said.

He looked at the house, surveying the damage. The tree had fallen across the extension that Geri's father had built to accommodate a new dining room. Though that extension was wrecked irreparably, the rest of the house was unharmed. It would provide the shelter they needed to get through the night *if* they could keep the flesh-lusting, darkness-seeking worms outside. Once they got through, Mick could drive at first light to the power company and get them to shut off the juice to Fly Creek till the downed line could be repaired.

"Where can I get some plywood to cover this hole before night?" he asked. "If I'm right, then the only thing keeping the worms back *is* the light."

"We don't have any," Geri said despairingly.

"What about a lumber yard?"

"There's nothing like that." Mick pounded his fist into the palm of bis hand, but then Geri remembered something. "There's an abandoned building in the woods. There's plenty of lumber there."

"Where is it?" Mick asked excitedly, hope rising again.

"I'll show you."

"She took him by the hand, but he planted his feet. No, you stay here. Your mother looks like she's about to crack. I'll be back as soon as possible. Stay in the house. And don't tell her about what we saw. And keep the candles burning." He looked into the darkness. "Which way?"

Geri thrust her chin in the direction of the woods to the south. Mick began to trot that way. "But how can you carry *it?*" she shouted after him.

"I'll think of something," he replied with more optimism than knowledge.

Chapter Fourteen

Geri tracked Mick into the woods until bis silhouette blended with the black shadows of night. She heard the snapping of twigs and brush in the distance, then there was only the sound of Georgia nighttime, the honking of bullfrogs, the cheeping and chirping of toads, and the riot of innumerable crickets. Wondering if she'd ever see Mick again, she turned and marched back to the house.

The living room glowed with the flickering light of half a dozen candles, and several more had been posted in the undamaged part of the dining room. Alma was busy picking up the smaller fragments of roofing material that littered the floor and stuffing them in a big trash bag she'd slung over her shoulder like a field hand picking cotton. Through the entrance to the living room Geri could see her mother, sitting on her favorite chair in the living room, uncomprehending eyes fixed on the fireplace mantle, mouth frozen in a meaningless smile.

It was, for Geri, a more distressing situation than if her mother were completely hysterical. Hysteria was at least a normal response to a catastrophe. It said, My circuits are over-loaded, I don't know whether to laugh or cry. But *this*—this almost catatonic stare...it wasn't healthy, it wasn't good. It seemed to indicate that her mother bad lost touch with every-thing, with her very emotions themselves. She was beyond laughing or crying. Geri felt a shiver. Her mother was in a dangerous state.

"Geri?" Mrs. Sanders reached out for her oldest daughter, gripping her hand almost savagely. "What's happening?"

Her mother's nails were like talons in Geri's flesh.

"The storm washed away the earth around the roots., That old tree just couldn't hold itself up anymore, that's all."

Mrs. Sanders' eyes roved the room slowly, like a pair of mechanical searchlights whose batteries have lost their potency. "Where's Mick?"

"He went to get some wood to cover up the hole temporarily for the night," Geri explained.

Mrs. Sanders nodded her head slowly, automatically. With growing concern Geri looked upon her mother's blank expres-sion. Try a diversion, Geri said to herself, until the woman can grasp what has happened. "Mother?" she said gaily. "I met Mrs. Norton today. She wanted to know if her shawl was ready."

Mrs. Sanders appeared to snap out of her trance for a moment. "It's almost finished. I nearly forgot."

Geri realized that knitting would be a good therapy for her mother. She reached behind her mother's chair and got out her sewing basket and a shopping bag filled with red and green wool, knitting needles, and a handsome red shawl with a green floral design. Only a corner remained to be done.

"Good. You work on the shawl. It'll steady your' nerves while I get the candles ready and clean up a little," said Geri. With more confidence, she left her mother and joined Alma in what was left of the dining room. Despite her youthful energy. Alma was fatigued by the work she'd done. Her eyes were glazed, her brow damp with sweat. Her shoulders were stooped beneath the weight of the trash bag filled with plaster and wood, and suddenly her knees buckled.

She dropped the sack and stood up, gasping. For a moment

she leaned against the trunk of the tree, panting. Then she staggered in the direction of the main house.

"Where are you going?" Geri snapped.

"To take a shower," Alma explained.

Geri sighed. "Okay. As long as you don't go outside."

Alma knew her sister intimately and was able to hear an ominous chord vibrating faintly in the tremor of Geri's voice. "What's outside?"

Geri flashed a high sign at Alma, gesturing with her head at their mother. The woman was just beginning to relax; set her off again and there was no telling what she would do. She was a rubber band twisted to its limits: she might snap, or she might untwist so violently she would twitch and bounce until she damaged herself dangerously.

Geri realized she'd panicked her sister unnecessarily. Trying to lighten the mood, she smiled playfully. "See if you have better luck than I did," she said, motioning with her chin at the upstairs bathroom. "There was no water at all before."

Alma took a fat candle on a plate and shuffled up the stairs. The dancing yellow flame flashed grotesque shadow patterns on the staircase wall, both fascinating and frightening the ascending girl. Wow! she said to herself, this trip should be taken with a headful of grass. It would be better than Walt Disney's *Fantasia*, which she'd seen after she and her friends had gotten sky-high on some stuff from Colombia that was ten times stronger than the Panama junk she'd been smoking. Oh, wow!

Her own shadow followed her into the bathroom and frolicked around the walls and ceiling like a taunting devil. Alma set the candle on the sink and leaned over the tub. She tried the faucets and was greeted by some obscene belches and gurgles from the pipes, but not so much as a drip of water. She looked up at the shower head, cursed, and kicked the side of the tub. It made a resounding hollow thump. but the gesture did more to hurt her toe than to produce water.

"Damn!"

She decided to leave the faucets in their open position. That way, when the water did come back on, she'd hear it and know she wouldn't have to wait till morning to clean the dust off her body and out of her hair.

She picked up the candle and went back downstairs.

The light was gone from the bathroom now. and the worms had nothing to inhibit them anymore. They slithered through the open valves of the shower faucets, up the pipes, and into the shower head, pushed by the tremendous pressure of hundreds of thousands of their brethren below. They found the shower head holes and squirmed through, wriggling until their tails were clear. For a moment they dropped through space, a detestable experience. Then they struck the hard cool porcelain of the bathtub. Shaking off the stunning impact, they tried to crawl up the sides of the tub, lured by the odor of human flesh that pervaded the house. But the walls were too steep, and they slipped and tumbled back onto the floor of the tub.

The platoon of worms that fell on top of them had better luck, for their plunges were cushioned by the worms that had already landed. Nor did they have as far to crawl to the top of the tub, because there was a half inch of worm-flesh beneath them.

The next wave of worms had even less distance to fall, and less to crawl.

With mounting excitement, the worms in the tub writhed, the prospects of invasion enhancing with each layer of worms that coated the last one. It was as if the mass of individuals had but one mind, one will, and one purpose, like the countless cells of the brain that constitute an intelligence higher by far than the sum of its constituent parts.

The tub filled slowly with worms, but for the worms, it didn't matter. What was time to them?

Chapter Fifteen

The deeper Mick got into the woods, the quieter it became. Perhaps this was a natural phenomenon, he said to himself, but he'd never heard of it. The only time the night creatures hushed their voices was when a storm was approaching.

Or danger lurked nearby.

Mick sensed it was the latter. The pricking of the skin on the nape of his neck told him something, somebody, was watching him. He wished he'd asked Geri what kind of dangerous animals inhabited the Georgia lowland forests. It was too far south for bear, he sup posed. But it was quite far south enough for alligators and moccasins, he remembered with a shiver.

Also mosquitoes, he added, clapping his neck with a cupped palm as one of the little demons bored into his flesh.

But mosquitoes wouldn't cause absolute quiet to fall over the woods.

There was something else afoot.

In the pit of his stomach he knew what it was, but his emotions were too fragile to bring the image before his mind's eye. His mind's eye blinked it away, sending it scurrying back into the hideous place in his imagination where such diabolical phantasms are spawned.

Mick was a pragmatist. He knew that the real thing, if and when it disclosed itself, would be horrible enough. Why scare himself with something imagined?

The night was still and hot, and mosquito-inviting sweat trickled over his brow, throat and neck.

In due course he came to a cleared patch, and in the dim blue light that filtered through the light cloud cover over the stars he perceived several piles of two-by-fours, a small mechanical cement mixer shaped like an inverted barrel, and a stack of eight-by-four plywood sheets. Mick ran his finger over the edge of one: it was half an inch thick. He frowned. He'd been hoping for a quarter inch. which God knows is heavy enough.

He pried two sheets away from the stack and cursed. More bad luck: the plywood was still soaked from last night's rain. Mick would not only be lugging all that wood; he'd be hauling the water that had swollen up its fiber as well.

He seized the plywood with his left hand on the bottom and his right on the top edge lengthwise and lifted. The plywood tilted over backward, indicating his bottom hand was too far forward. He made the adjustment and hefted the plywood again. This time it balanced perfectly on the fulcrum of the heel of his left hand. His right hand simply kept the boards upright as he aimed himself in the direction from whence he'd come and began his return to the Sanders' home with a staggering gait.

As he counted out twenty paces before pantingly putting the boards down to rest, all he could do was pray that there would be no wind. A wind would strike the plywood boards like the topsail of a square-rigged ship and, with his luck running as it had been all day, carry him to somewhere off the coast of Bermuda.

His labored breathing as he paused for his first rest was the only sound in the woods, and without any other noises to contrast with it was enough to make the dead. Waking the dead was something Mick had little desire to do, tonight of all nights.

He was about to pick up the plywood for his second twenty-yard rush when he heard the crack of a small twig snapping, as if beneath the weight of a heavy creature.

Mick's heart thundered in his chest cavity. After complaining about the deathly silence of these woods, he would have been very happy to get that deathly silence back again. He tried to judge the direction from which the noise had come, but it seemed to have no locus. He cocked his ear for a full minute, but whatever it was out there wouldn't oblige him by making another noise.

The best thing to do was pick up the plywood again and make a dash for the house, a sprint of a quarter of a mile or so, awkwardly lugging over a hundred pounds of waterlogged plywood. Sure. Easy. If you're a forklift truck.

He bent at the knees and put his back into lifting the boards up. Trotting sideways, like a sailboat before a breeze off the starboard beam, Mick stepped off five, ten, fifteen paces.

As he stepped off the next five he heard, Oh God, a second pair of feet He looked forward, backward, and over his shoulder behind him, but made out nothing in the pitch-dark night. Naturally not, he reflected because if *I* were going to attack someone running through the woods carrying plywood boards, I'd take him from his blind side—four feet by eight feet worth of it.

That was Mick's next-to-last reflection. The very last reflection before the thing hurled itself against the plywood (from Mick's blind side, of course) was, Oh Lord, let it be simply the owner of the lumber coming after me to get his plywood back. How happily Mick would welcome some gruff voice hurling epithets at him for removing building materials without permission. He'd gladly let his attacker keep the five years of life Mick had just lost in fright anyway, and he'd throw two pieces of plywood and his butane lighter into the bargain.

But it was not the owner of the lumber come to reclaim his property. It was another human. But scarcely.

Roger's throat uttered a bloodcurdling sound somewhere between a Rebel yell and the bray of a beast in unspeakable pain. He flung himself against the plywood with such force that his shoulder and hip splintered it, knocking Mick backward over the edge of a muddy gully. He plunged down the almost sheer slope about fifteen feet, somersaulting the last five and coming down awkwardly on top of his own ankle. A violent pain radiated from the ankle outward, like thin ice shattering beneath a heavy boot-heel, and for an instant the night was lit up with a million pinpoints of pain.

Mick tried to get to his feet but the bottom of the gully was sloshy with mud, and his ankle was badly' twisted if not broken. He peered up to the lip of the gully and in the faint light suffusing the world through the thin cloud layer above, made out a figure dancing like an elated ape. "Geri is mine!" Roger screamed triumphantly. "She always was. You had to come and spoil everything. Now we'll see what *you* look like after the worms get *you!*"

Mick stared in horrified fascination at the face of the tormentor above. May I never seen anything so ghastly again, Mick prayed silently as he witnessed the remains of a face punctured through and through as if with bullets, except that out of each puncture hole a tail tip wiggled. Black bloodstains mottled what remained of Roger's face, but his round eyes glowed yellow even in this darkness, and his white teeth shone like the Cheshire Cat's, but evilly.

Suddenly the sky behind Roger's head was blotted out, and it took Mick a moment to figure out what the rectangular shape was that was eclipse the night sky.

It was Mick's plywood. Roger had lifted a piece and was about to hurl it down upon his victim. The first piece sang in the air as it hurtled to within an inch of Mick's legs. He scrambled awkwardly in the mud with his one good ankle dragging the bad one. The plywood landed on its short side, hovered for a moment, then fell harmlessly on Mick's shoulder.

If only he could avoid the second piece successfully too!

No, Mick said to himself, eyes rounding as Roger raised the other board over his head, it'll never happen. Not the way my luck has been running today.

He was right.

The edge of the board glanced the back of his skull, but a board that heavy thrown from that distance doesn't glance your skull without taking a large portion of your consciousness with it.

The pressure of the rampaging worms was too much for the shower head in the Sanders' bathroom. It finally shattered and fell into the living cauldron of worms in the tub below. No longer did the shower look like a meat grinder turning out discrete lengths of purple flesh; it now looked like an open aqueduct out of which flowed an endless molten mass of the stuff, moving at the rate that honey pours out of a jar. The worms had almost filled the tub and already the first phalanxes had gone over the top and were wriggling blindly for living space. They had found their way into the plumbing of the sink as well and were surging through the faucet. They came up through the pipe that led into the toilet tank and were issuing from that aperture at a slow but steady rate. In due time the top of the tank began to rattle with the activity of the thousands of creatures crowding against it demanding their freedom...free-dom...freedom...

Downstairs Geri had opened another faucet, this one belonging to the kitchen sink. She held a glass under the tap, hoping to coax just enough water out of it to quench her parched throat. Worry and fright had raised a patina of perspiration on her face and body, and the still heat of the night only aggravated it.

Upstairs a sound....

Mrs. Sanders, sitting in her favorite chair in the living room, knitting in the dark, heard it too. "Alma? Geri? Did you hear a noise?"

"No, Mother." Geri looked at Alma. "Bring her a candle," Geri ordered.

Alma had heard it too, and thought she recognized the sound of the porcelain toilet tank top, a sound she knew all too well from the many times she'd fixed the darned gurgling flush apparatus. Whatever it was, it spooked her, and she trembled merely to cross the darkened space between kitchen and living room.

She picked up her own candle in a dish, and another for her mother, and tiptoed into the living room, breathing deeply to drive the stale air of fear out of her lungs, forcing her mouth to bloom in a cheerful smile.

The shadows of her own self, cast in duplicate on the wall and ceiling (one for each candle) played cruel tricks on her imagination as she walked deliberately across the threshold of the living room. Her mother sat in her chair, looking very pale and drawn, her hands flicking their knitting needles like the mechanical parts of an automaton. The wool slithered wormlike out of the ball in the bag and twined itself around the metal needles, to be artfully hooked and knotted into the design by hands that seemed to know the way without the assistance of a brain.

It was creepy, thought Alma. Her mother looked like a zombie.

"Look who's talking about reading in the dark," Alma joked.

Her mother heard no joke. She only heard that rattling. "Did you hear it?"

"No," Alma breathed. "Mother, don't scare me."

They sat silently, heads cocked. Now the rattling of porcelain was replaced by a sort of hissing, flowing sound, hard to identify. "Did you leave the water running in the bathroom?" Mrs. Sanders asked.

Suddenly Alma beamed. Of course! That was it! She'd left the faucets open in the shower so that when the water finally did come up, she'd hear it. "Yeah. Oh wow!" She jumped to her feet. "Geri, the water's coming out upstairs!" She bounded to the foot of the stairs. "I can't wait to wash my face."

"Be careful, honey," Mrs. Sanders cautioned. "It's very dark up there."

Alma put on the brakes. Her mother was right. No sense in breaking your neck just because you're dying to dive into the shower. She returned for a candle, then padded up the stairs.

As she did she frowned and tilted her head, her ears focusing on the sound. It was odd: that was not the sound of running water. It was the sound of running *something*, but what the heck could it be?

Holding the candle with her left hand, she stopped outside the bathroom door and tested the knob with her right. The door pushed against her shoulder, as if a strong wind was trying to blow it open. She put her shoulder to the door, some profound instinct telling her to beware of whatever it was on the other side. She allowed the door to open one controlled fraction of an inch.

A nine-inch worm wriggled out, straining for Alma's toes.

Startled and revolted, she raised her foot and slammed it down on the worm, sending a ribbon of guts shooting across the floor.

But to do this she had to relax her grip against the door.

The door sprang open, giving Alma just enough time to confront what it was on the other side. An avalanche of slimy living flesh poured out of the door, engulfing and submerging her and stifling her scream before it could exit from her throat. She swam through the roiling mass of disgust, gasping for air, grasping for a fingerhold on anything more solid than worms.

Her fingers found only more worm.

She was drowning in a sea of them. Drowning...

Downstairs, Geri waited anxiously for Mick to return. She felt as if she'd never been lonelier or more frightened in her life. Alma was upstairs somewhere; Mick was off in the woods; and Mother—Mother was as good as gone. The woman went through the paces of being human, but the light had gone out of her eyes, as if her soul had vacated her body. as if her brain had been lobotomized, leaving a scarf-knitting robot in the place of the woman who had nurtured her two daughters.

She noticed the candle that she'd left in the debris of the dining room guttering. It had used up its wax and was just about out. It must be replaced at once. She took a lighted candle off the fireplace mantle and carried it into the ravaged dining area. The other candle had gone out. She could see the fading red dot of the wick and smell the strangely pleasant but pungent smoke of the extinguished candle. She stooped to set the replacement on the floor.

Out of the comer of her eye she noticed something advancing toward her. For a second, she thought it was just a shadow. for the candle played strange visual tricks with common objects, making hands look as large and ominous on a wall as vultures, and a begonia growing on a table inside the kitchen look like a giant man-eating plant.

So, this shadow creeping steadily across the dining room floor toward her feet, even though it looked like an army of worms in this tricky candlelight, would surely reveal itself to be something ridiculously ordinary when she looked at it more closely.

Her blood froze as she brought the candle closer. Fortunately, the candlelight checked the forward movement of the worm-troops. They retreated before the light, and Geri, despite a revulsion so profound she wanted to spew her guts, had the presence of mind to charge them with the candle. They reversed their liquid flow and slinked off into the darkness.

Geri bit her hand, fighting back nausea and panic. As long

as she left the candle where it was, she reasoned, the worms would hold their position. Now, if she could round up enough candles to last till morning's first light, she and her family could survive the siege.

"Mother, where's Alma?" she demanded, returning to the living room.

"Upstairs," the woman said in singsong voice, knitting needles clicking.

Geri wasn't sure that this meant Alma was necessarily safe, but there was a more immediate concern. "Is the front door closed?"

"Yes," her mother said, "but I left the back open to get some fresh air. I wish there was a breeze," she sighed.

Oh God no! Geri's mind screamed as she raced to the door that opened on the back yard. Fortunately, Alma had left a candle on the hall table beside the door, which served to keep the worms at bay.

She put her hand on the knob and was about to shut it when a human shadow loomed up on the hall wall. It was not her own.

"Mick? Is that you?"

No, it was not Mick.

It was Roger.

What was left of Roger.

Her knees buckled as the ghoulish figure clapped a hand on her mouth and with the other hand, with half a thumb and forefinger, pinched out the flame of the candle. Geri writhed in the powerful embrace of her captor, but his strength was overwhelming. He reeked of the ammoniac odor of worm droppings, clotted blood. fear and stale perspiration.

Geri had never fainted in her life but there was a first time, she heard her mind say, for everything. Whatever was going to happen to her, it was just as well she was unconscious when it happened.

In the living room Mrs. Sanders smiled and held the shawl

up to the dim flicker of the candle. "There," she said to Geri, who she believed was within range of her voice, "Mrs. Norton would love this for herself, if only she wasn't allergic to wool, poor dear. All I have to do is block it and I'll be through."

Now, what did I do with those scissors, Naomi Sanders asked herself, groping around her knitting box and the bag of wool at her feet. No; not there. Ah, the shelf behind her. She reached up and explored the shelf with blind fingers.

A dozen worms rested on it. Smelling the attractive aroma of human flesh, they attacked.

Her hand found the scissors a mere second before the worms found her hand. For that moment she was out of danger.

But for that moment only. Above her head, unknown to her, the ceiling was alive with them. The pressure of the falling elm had weakened an already weak spot, and the hunger of the troops of worms had accomplished the rest. They marched like victorious soldiers through the rough stucco, forming a gaping tear which allowed more and more of them to enter above the head of the unsuspecting Mrs. Sanders.

And now, like a paratroop invasion, they began to drop off, landing around her feet and creeping up the legs of the chair. As she started to snip the strand of wool from the finished shawl, her chair seemed to burst into life. She sat in a living chair. A living chair of death.

Chapter Sixteen

Irene Anderson clung to Sheriff Reston's arm as he fumbled with his keys. "My goodness," she drawled," you sure do have a lot of keys on that chain."

"There's only one key that counts, little lady," he grinned, "and that's the key to your heart."

"Oh, I think you've already found that one," she giggled. He'd certainly behaved like a perfect gentleman from the moment she'd approached him that morning. Her car had all but run out of gas in Fly Creek, but the man at the gas station was unable to refill her tank because the electricity that operated the pump was off. Could the sheriff help her?

Well, the sheriff couldn't help her as far as gas was concerned, but he'd be more than happy to make her unforeseen stay in Fly Creek just as painless as possible, he'd said. And he had. He'd bought her lunch, presented her with a pretty necklace, taken her to dinner, plied her with wine, joked and teased her. She'd guessed what accommodation he had in mind for her one night stay in Fly Creek, but that was all right. It wasn't as if he was some sweaty redneck pawing her and breathing alcohol and cigar tobacco down her neck. This was a gentleman. He had played the game exactly the way a lady likes the game to be played, and if he now expected a reward, she was not disinclined to bestow one on him. After all, she laughed to herself, it's not as if she hated sleeping with a man, exactly.

"Ah, here we go," Sheriff Reston. said, inserting a brass key into a cell door on the third floor of the courthouse. It's not much but it's comfortable," he added, looking at the cot.

"A bed is a bed; now isn't that right, Jim?" she said, smiling coyly. She sat down on the bed and patted the place next to her. "I'm mighty tired, Jim, mighty tired."

Sheriff Reston knew enough to understand that Irene's use of the word tired was not meant to be taken literally.

He sat down and removed his Stetson, flung it across the room. She raised her face and he pressed his lips to hers. She murmured and yielded to his importuning lips. Her breasts heaved as he drew her body close to his and caressed her ardently. She fell back, arms extended to her lover, who covered her body with his beefy weight, grinning his pelvis against hers. The hunger swelled between them like the rising chords of a symphony finale. They paused to shed their clothing. Reston's eyes dined on her voluptuous figure as she bent over the bed and pulled back the sheet.

She finished smoothing the sheets, then lay down, and beckoned to him. Reston finished undressing and kicked his jodhpurs into a dusty corner. "Ready or not," he said, grinning.

"Oh, I'm ready, sweetie," she said. "I'm plenty ready."

They lost track of time, but it seemed they made love for hours. She was fierce and animal in her passion, bringing out a lust and stamina in him that he rarely had a chance to display. In due time the candle sputtered, crackled, and extinguished.

They lay quietly in each other's arms. Then they had a hankering for a cigarette, and Reston tiptoed across the room to fetch his pack out of his shirt pocket. Unknown to him, a river of worms had crept up the plumbing of the little water closet next to his makeshift love-nest, and was closing in on the shirt which lay strewn across a chair. His feet narrowly missed the advance guard, which squirmed in anticipation of the flesh it craved.

He returned to the bed, put two cigarettes in his mouth. and struck a match. The mass of invading worms surrounding the bed hesitated, and one wave retreated against the door, causing it to rattle.

"What was that?" Irene asked, pulling the sheets up around her.

The sheriff tilted his head but scoffed. "Don't worry. I have the key," he assured her. He handed her a lighted cigarette and they inhaled deeply, blowing the smoke into the air sibilantly. All the light in the room focused around those two red glowing ashes on the ends of their cigarettes.

Irene giggled. "Stop doing that."

Reston frowned. He wasn't touching her. "Doing what?"

She giggled again. "That."

Reston shifted to his side and looked at her peculiarly. Her eyes were closed and she was sighing softly, as if anticipating another session in the sheriff's arms. "I'm not doing anything.".

Irene's eyes opened and she gazed at him in mounting terror. Then she brought her knees to her chest in sudden agony and screamed. For a moment Reston thought, oh God, another crazy dame. Then the first of the bloodsucking worms attached itself to his little toe, and he knew that something awful was in bed with them.

A moment later they saw what it was, but by that time their mattress was aswarm with them. and their screams echoed ineffectively in the night until the worms smothered their voices....

The hysterical shrieks from the third floor of the courthouse barely carried across the street to Quigley's, but they were detected above the blare of the transistor radio by Eddie. With Jeff, Susanne, and Amy, he sat at the Formica table by the window, head nodding drunkenly, when the terrible cries penetrated his booze-fogged brain.

"Did you hear that?"

Susanne raised her head. and opened the lids of her eyes. "What?"

Eddie drew his bayonet out of its scabbard and made a pathetic gesture of gallantry. "Give me that candle," he said, rising uncertainly to his feet.

Jeff pulled out of his stupor just long enough to hand the candle to his pal. Then he nodded off again like a guest at the Mad Hatter's Tea Party.

Looking a good deal less than a cavalry officer about to lead a do-or-die charge across no-man's land, Eddie raised the bayonet and dashed out on the floor of the bar.

He slid about three feet in the slime of ten thousand worms that had burst into the room through the kitchen, consuming the cook and everything else edible. Until Eddie set foot on the floor, nobody else in the bar knew of the menace in their midst because they sat above it on their stools.

When Eddie plunged into the sea of worms, however, they learned. His cries and blubbers were dreadful to hear, and it was quickly apparent that they were not the sounds of someone who'd had too much to drink. They were the sounds of death.

But before anyone could come to Eddie's rescue, those same sounds were issuing from the throats of all the other patrons. In the first minutes eight or ten went down beneath the slinking death at their feet. A few climbed on top of the bar, figuring they were safely above the danger.

Until the first contingent of ceiling worms began dropping into their hair....

Chapter Seventeen

For several moments Mick hadn't the slightest idea where he was or what had happened to him. He had only the evidence of his senses to guide him, and that wasn't much help. His senses told him it was a dark night, that he was outdoors, that he lay in muddy earth, that there was a large piece of plywood partially covering his body, that his head hurt and his leg was killing him.

He lay still, listening to the chirp of a solitary cricket, until his brain began to weave together the information gathered from his senses and restore his memory. When it did come back it almost overloaded his mind. He pushed the plywood board off with a grunt, then sat up with a start. He was at the bottom of a steeply inclined pit whose walls contained just enough rocks, roots, and ledges to give him purchase—or rather, to give purchase to a man with two good legs. But Mick's right ankle, where he'd sat on it hard after Roger tossed him into the pit, felt broken. Getting up that incline with one leg would prove a more challenging test of Mick's outdoorsmanship than anything he'd bargained on when he'd climbed aboard the New York-Miami bus... when was it? Yesterday? Yesterday? So much had happened in such a short time that seconds and minutes and hours lost their meaning.

He winced, struggling to his feet. It all came back to him now. Roger. Worms. *Worms!* Roger had threatened something about worms when he'd knocked Mick into the pit.

Mick plunged his hand into his pocket and produced his butane lighter.

He flicked it igniting a tall flame. Must conserve fuel, Mick said to himself, twisting the tiny control knob until the flame shrank to a quarter of an inch. He held it up to the steep muddy walls of the pit and beheld a thousand wriggling heads, snatching at the night air from inside their miniature caves in the mud. They shrank and wiggled back into their holes before the flame of Mick's lighter.

He knew, though, that the dim glow wouldn't be enough to hold the creatures at bay while he attempted to scale the wall of the pit. He could feel ten thousand eyes on him, waiting. An errant gust of wind while he climbed and it would be all over. The remembrance of Roger's worm-eaten face was enough to inspire Mick to prodigies of ingenuity.

He held the lighter up and scanned the floor of the pit. Stuck in the mud about a yard away from him was a tree branch about two feet long. He picked it up. then set it by his feet, carefully placing the lighter in an upright position beside it. Now his hands were free, and he quickly unbuttoned his shirt and stripped out of it.

He picked up the stick and wrapped his shirt around the end of it, knotting it like a turban with the sleeves. Then he picked up his lighter and held the flame beneath the shirt. The shirt flared into blue flame.

He dropped the lighter back into his pocket and hoisted the torch over his head.

Just in time.

He looked down at his feet. The worms had formed an attack perimeter of a yard around his toes. He thrust the torch at them and they cleared an exit path like the Red Sea parting before Moses' command. He limped up the wall of the pit and peered at it. Before the intense glow of his torch, the cave dwellers retreated deep into the earth.

There was no time to lose. His shirt would consume itself in flame within minutes.

He found a gnarled root about four feet off the floor of the pit, and, grasping it and placing his good foot on a narrow rock ledge, hauled himself up. He stood on the ledge, surveying the next handhold in the light of his torch. He rested one rock, but it came out of the earth and tumbled to the pit below. Another one held steady and he hoisted himself to another yard. He quickly became drenched in sweat. The effort of boosting himself up the incline with one bad leg and one hand—the other held the torch—was the most difficult of his life.

Two more tries ought to do it.

He mapped out his route. There was a big rock about two feet over his head, then the roots of a pine tree that grew on the rim of the pit. He fingered the smooth rock until he found a niche and…yes! Up he went, his good foot found a ledge and he was within reach of the lip of the *pit*. His hand enclosed the tree root. It was high above him, too high to haul himself out with one hand alone. But without the torch…

He waved the torch around the wall of the pit and the rim, hoping to drive back any potential attackers far enough so that by the time they could advance again he'd have scaled the last part of the wall. Then he tossed the torch over the top. grabbed the root with both hands and shinned himself up, kicking at the soil with his good foot. He could hear himself grunting and cursing and for a second his muscles failed him. Then his imagination conjured the wounds of an army of maddened worms burrowing into the meat of his calf and thigh, and he shot out of the pit as if someone had goosed him. There was nothing to get the old adrenaline pumping like the fear of being eaten by worms, he declared to himself, almost laughing.

He picked up the torch. surveyed the ground, and found another dead branch, crooked but serviceable as a cane. Fighting the sharp pain in his ankle, he limped back toward the house, his heart thundering in dread of what he might find there.

His torch had all but extinguished itself as he broke into the clearing around the Sanders' house, and his stomach churned as he realized he could detect no light in the windows. That was bad, very bad.

He limped to the wreckage of the dining room, picked through it cautiously, and stepped inside the house. "Geri? Anybody here?"

He held the torch in front of him and sucked his breath in, horrified to the marrow of his bones. A river of worms flowed through the breach in the building's wall, forming a delta of worms in the kitchen, and beyond it an open sea of worms in the living room. More horrible than any nightmare, this living Sargasso boiled like a thick soup. When the front ranks shrank before his torch, they sent a wave through the sea of worms like an ocean swell.

Waving his torch around his feet, Mick stepped in, proceeding one foot at a time and being careful to thrust the firebrand behind his heels to hold back the tide that flowed in his footsteps.

Just as the flame began to flicker, he found a couple of candles on a kitchen counter. Beside it, a box of wooden matches. He lit the candles, then hurled the expiring torch into the sink. Then he picked up the candles, one in each hand. and waved them in a circle around his body, stooping close to the floor. Ripples radiated across the seething floor like heavy stones dropped in a pond.

Mick placed a cautious foot in the spot vacated by the worms and held a candle in front of him to clear a path while holding the other candle behind him to keep the backwash of snapping jaws from flowing in over his heels. Thus, he moved deliberately toward the living room, dreading to see what might be there, yet dreading just much not knowing what had become of Geri and Alma and their mother.

He discovered, at least, what had happened to their mother. The sight was so revolting he gagged and retched and felt he was going to pass out.

In Mrs. Sanders' favorite chair sat a skeleton. It wore Mrs. Sanders' dress. Its head was covered with Mrs. Sanders' luxuriant dark hair. Its shoes were those in which he'd last seen Mrs. Sanders. In its lap was the shawl Mrs. Sanders had been knitting. The bony fingers of the skeleton still clutched the knitting needles, though the skein of wool leading to the bag at her feet was indistinguishable from the skein of worms that busied itself on the bits of flesh that still clung to her leg. Her dress rippled as the starving creatures devoured what was left of her breasts and belly and thighs, her heart and lungs and intestines and liver and pancreas. A few worms pecked at the remaining skin of her lips and the cartilage that had been her nose, and a few slimy fibers that had once been her eyes.

"Oh no," Mick whimpered, shutting his eyes.

But he had no time for mourning. Even in the instant he'd shut his eyes, the attacking worms had surged forward, challenging the candlelight, seemingly prepared to sacrifice some of their numbers in the hopes of tackling their prey, like charging Asian troops to whom the loss of a few thousand lives is meaningless. Mick held the candles at floor level, sweeping his arms around in clockwise and counterclockwise motions to open a path to the stairs, which were free of worms, but slippery with excreta.

He leaped two feet to the first step, taking care to protect the candle flames from being blown out. Then he made his way up to the first landing. Looking behind him, he witnessed the sea of worms in the living room rising fast like the estuary of a river, fed by a flow through the breach in the dining room wall where the tree had fallen. He estimated five or ten thousand worms were pouring into the house each minute. Already they were two or three feet deep. He had just escaped. If he were to return now, even with candles, they were too deep to be able to clear a path for him. There was absolutely no place for them to go.

He walked carefully to Geri's room. The door was open. He held a candle before him and poked his head in. "Geri? Alma?" the room was empty.

He peered into Alma's room. Empty too.

A trail of slime and detritus led out of the bathroom and down the stairs, but the bathroom was now free of worms.

He had to work fast. With the living room filling up fast, and with the odor of human flesh in their nostrils, the worms would soon be slithering their way up the stairs. He had to find the girls quickly or abandon his search and flee for a safe place.

Then he remembered the attic. He looked at the ladder and saw what seemed to be fresh mud. He set one candle on the floor to protect his rear, and with the other guided himself up the ladder. Two rungs. Three. Four. Two more to go.

Roger struck so fast Mick never really saw it coming. His hands fired out of the black hole, one grabbing Mick's hair, the other his arm. In that instant, as if time itself had frozen in horror, Mick saw the face of death itself. How Roger had managed to go on living with his worm-eaten face and brain, Mick could not imagine. The bone of the skull was visible where his cheeks and mouth had been. Half of his ears were gone, and the bony plate of his forehead glistened in the orange light. Apparently no worms had penetrated deeply enough into his brain to perpetrate the *coup de grace*. One worm had, however, eaten through Roger's tongue and wriggled head and tail at right angles to the tortured organ.

Seeing that, Mick was sure he screamed, but he never heard himself. Roger's clutch on his hair and arm was savage, the death grip of a man who, has nothing left to lose and lives only to bring as many to doom with him as he can.

They were eyeball-to-eyeball when Mick, snapping out of

his paralysis, shoved the candle into Roger's face. It was a last ditch move, and Mick was pretty doubtful that anybody whose face was eaten through by worms would feel the pain of a flame-burn on his cheek. Luckily Mick was wrong. Roger flinched and relaxed his grip enough to allow Mick to wrench free. So doing, Mick toppled backward onto the floor.

In the process, the candle in his hand went out—and he landed on the candle on the floor.

Utter darkness. Mick knew only the location of the enemy. One was swirling and seething tormentedly up the stairs. The other was preparing to leap upon him from above. Mick braced himself for the latter, and just in time. Roger's heavy right boot kicked Mick in the shoulder, but Mick managed to grab a leg and haul Roger off balance. Roger snatched at Mick's ear as he tumbled to the second-floor landing, and Mick was certain the animal had pulled it off his head. Blindly Mick swung both fists, bidding for the time he needed for his eyes to adjust to the dark. One fist missed entirely, the other caught Roger in the throat. Roger bellowed like a wounded beast and slumped to the floor.

For a minute there was no sound but the seething of the blood lusting worms downstairs, like a rumbling of a high sea on the shore on an angry night. From the few glints of fugitive light seeping in through the windows, Mick could see the first turbulent units of the worm armies mounting the third or fourth step of the stairs.

Mick reached into his pocket and produced his butane lighter and the matches he'd found downstairs. The lighter flicked twice, three times, but failed. He chucked it into the vortex of the worms downstairs, where it plopped and disappeared immediately as if into a pool of bubbling tar.

He tried a match with shaking hands and it flared into light.

He looked for Roger.

He found him—charging like a lust-crazed ram. Mick had just enough time to brace his abdomen for the impact. The wind only went half out of him, which was enough. More significant, the impact sent him spraddling backward to the edge of the landing. He managed to grab a banister brace as he slid over the edge of the top stair, checking the fall which would have been his last.

In a flash Roger was on top of him, flailing with fists, elbows, knees, feet, and even teeth in a final desperate offensive, a Battle of the Bulge, the bulge being Mick himself as he clutched the banister for all he was worthwhile taking every blow that Roger could rain on him.

Roger must have realized that the only way to effectively dispose of Mick was to pry loose Mick's fingers and toss him down into the hissing mass below. Mick was puzzled by the moment's hiatus in the awful thrashing, for in another few seconds he would have lost consciousness. Then it came to him: Roger was going to kick his fingers.

He pulled his fingers away just as the boot swished through the air. Roger's foot cut an arc between two banister braces and he shinned himself on the banister itself. Mick, as much to keep his balance as anything else, grasped for Roger's leg and got it and held it like a drowning man. Roger brayed and kicked, trying to make Mick release his foot. Mick would no sooner have done that than volunteered to swan-dive into the worms below.

Frantic, Roger stooped over to pry Mick's hands loose from his leg. He lost his balance and waved his hands like a semaphore signalman. In that fraction of an instant when Roger hovered over the stairs, Mick felt a strange compassion. This man wanted to destroy him, yet Mick could not allow him to suffer the horrible fate that lay below. Mick grabbed for his shoe but missed as Roger tumbled past him and somersaulted head-first into the living, teeming sea below.

Mick was too busy scrambling for safety to see it all, but he heard the enormous *PLOP* as Roger fell like a belly whopper on the surface, then a sucking noise as he submerged. The five-foot-thick bed of worms convulsed as a single individual, like a starved beast sinking its teeth into a large chunk of raw meat. When Mick finally gained his foothold, he looked over his shoulder to see Roger submerged to the neck, his face a portrait of unmitigated pain. He flailed with his arms as if trying feebly to wade back toward the stairs, looking like a swimmer walking out of the sea against an outrushing wave.

Mick turned away. Several times today he'd felt his gorge rise and this time it all but overwhelmed him. He swallowed back bitter acid, rose shakily to his feet. And wobbled to the foot of the ladder, where he found one of the candles and relit it.

Rung by rung he ascended the ladder, muscles tensed either to propel him forward for attack or backward for retreat, depending on what he found up there. Suppose Geri was up there, maddened by brain-devouring worms as Roger had been. Would he be able to watch passively as she sank beneath the roiling surface of a sea of worms, to be indifferent to her agony as twenty thousand little fangs buried themselves into every pore on her body?

Cautiously he raised the candle into the blackness of the attic and peered over the top.

Geri lay on her stomach, arms and legs tied together behind her back; mouth gagged.

She was alive.

There were no worms up here. Yet.

He rushed to her and loosened the gag and ropes. "Are you all right?"

For a second, she just gasped, nodding her head. Then she fell into his arms, panting and weeping quietly. Mick held her tenderly for a moment, wishing he could do this for the rest of the night. But a rumble from below reminded him that there would be no respite. The worms were throwing division after division into their assault, as the Vandals and Goths must have done once the walls of Rome were breached. Soon they would arrive at the second floor and would probably advance on the third.

He rushed to the window in the attic and raised it. "I can't see a damn thing." That wasn't completely true.

In the bluish aura of starlight that filtered through the thin cloud cover, he could see the ground below—except it wasn't ground Geri rummaged through a chest of drawers and found a flashlight for him. He shined it out the window onto the ground.

His fear was confirmed.

There was no ground. It was worms, worms too numerous to count, worms too numerous even to conceive of. The world was worms. No prophet of doom. Biblical or modern, had ever faintly imagined that the world might end this way. But it appeared to be happening.

He turned his light on an object near the window. "How are you at climbing trees?" he said. A limb ran close to the window.

Geri nodded distractedly, but she was looking down the trap door. Her face was distorted with apprehension. "Mick, where's Alma? And my mother?"

She seemed to shudder and Mick realized she was on the verge of hysteria. He took her tightly by the shoulders. "You can't go down there. The worms are halfway up the stairs already. We have to get out of here. *Now!*"

Geri shook her head and tried to free herself from Mick's hold. "No, I have to help them. Let me go."

She struggled with surprising ferocity, but Mick was determined to clutch her until her grief passed. "It's too late," he finally yelled. "They're dead!" It was cruel but it was the only course under the circumstances. Geri gave one last convulsive jerk, then went limp. She buried her face in her hands and began sobbing.

He carried her to the window and helped her onto the limb outside. It swayed precariously and dipped at an angle that made Mick wonder gravely about its ability to support two people. Well— he'd find out soon enough.

He grasped the limb with one hand and hurled one leg over

the windowsill. He was about to boost himself out when he heard a shuffle on the attic floor behind him. He turned just in time to see—oh God, that eyes were made to see *this!—the* form of Roger staggering toward him. It was only a form. There were no features recognizable as human. There were only worms. It was a human-shaped mass of worms. They hung in festoons from his outstretched arms.

Roger's hand enclosed Mick's arm as Mick rushed back into the room to confront the menace squarely. He shook his arm loose and brought the flashlight down with all his might on Roger's head. The first blow was cushioned by the layer of worms on his scalp and didn't seem to deter this monster, but Mick struck again, and again, and again.

His grip relaxed. Then he released Mick and slumped to the floor. His body twitched horribly as the worms bored into his brain and heart. Then he ceased to move.

Mick brushed several worms off his wrist and all but dove out the window to the limb of the tree. It dipped precariously and cracked, and in a night of terrifying noises this was by for the most terrifying. Mick could almost feel the million jaws of death fastening on his hide as he plummeted into the bed of forms at the base of the tree. But the branch held and he scrambled closer to the crotch of the tree where Geri sat huddled, eyes bugged with the terrors she had endured and still endured.

Mick beamed the flashlight at the foot of the tree to discourage any assault up the trunk. He remembered those ads for long-lasting flashlight batteries that had carried stranded campers through nights of danger. He hoped that brand of battery was in his flashlight, and that the advertiser's claims were true. It must be early morning. There was still plenty of darkness left, and no end of worms waiting to take advantage of failing batteries.

Chapter Eighteen

After what they had been through, cramped limbs seemed like a minor nuisance and a cheap price to pay for survival. Like a pair of squirrels stretching after a storm, Mick and Geri untwined and tested their arms and legs. The sun shone bright and warm in their eyes.

They looked down. Except for the flattened grass and a thin pebbly layer of worm-leavings, there was no sign that anything had happened at all. At first light the worms had retreated into the bowels of the earth from whence they had come.

"Hey-uh, excuse me?"

They looked down at the friendly face of a man in a work uniform, yellow helmet, and utility belt. There was a GP&L emblem on his sleeve—Georgia Power and Light.

"I thought you two love birds might want to know that the power's back on. Tower's all fixed up, good as new."

Mick and Geri stared dumbly at him. He returned the stare at the couple sitting for no apparent reason in a tree.

"Oh, by the way—which way's town?" Mick pointed in the direction of Fly Creek.

"I hope they got some nice hot coffee ready," he said, ambling back to his truck. Then he stopped. "Strangest thing.

All the lines are back up but nobody seems to be answering the damn phones around here." He got back into his truck and waved goodbye. "Damn nice place," he said to himself, starting the engine. "Wouldn't mind livin' around here."

Geri and Mick descended and entered the house. The destruction wreaked by the worms was fantastic. In her mother's chair sat the skeleton of Naomi Sanders, in repose. Geri looked at it but could make no association with the human that had been her mother. And perhaps that was just as well.

They ascended the staircase, still slippery with the slime of a million worms. They reached the second floor and looked around the storage room, bedrooms, and bathrooms. There was no sign of...

Suddenly there was a squeak, like a badly oiled hinge opening. It came from the direction of the huge steamer trunk outside the bathroom. Mick tensed, looking for a weapon.

Then two platform shoes emerged from the trunk, followed by the legs and bedraggled body of Alma. She smiled a crooked smile, and the three embraced.

They went outside and stood in the sun, warming themselves. The world sparkled like an emerald in its bright light.

They said a silent prayer for Mrs. Sanders and the others who had perished in this freak of malevolent nature. Then they went back into the house again to pick up the pieces of their lives.

An AVALANCHE of KILLER WORMS
...writhing across the land in a tidal wave of terror!
Starts WEDNESDAY
an American
International
Release
SQUIRM
R RESTRICTED
THE EDGAR LANSBURY JOSEPH BERUH Presents
'SQUIRM' DON SCARDINO PATRICIA PEARCY R.A. DOW JEAN SULLIVAN
Are they DEMONS beyond God or man?
THEY CAME FROM WITHIN
Color prints by Movielab • a TRANS-AMERICAN FILMS Release R
ENDS TUES.
"Pom Pom Girls"
ALSO
"Swinging Cheerleaders"
OPEN 8:30
GRAND ISLAND
DRIVE IN TWIN 1
THEATRE

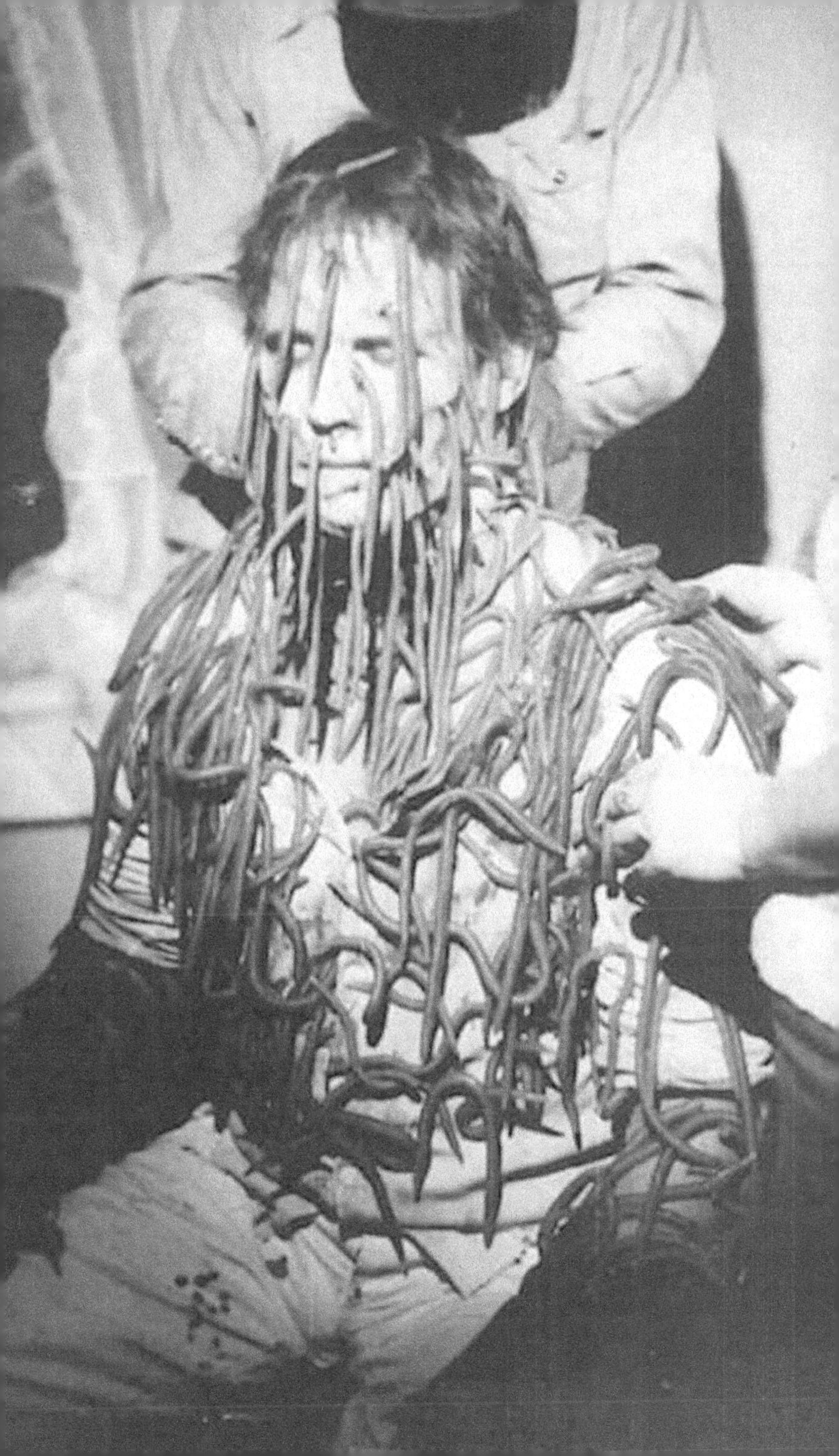

A NIGHT OF CRAWLING TERROR!
Squirm
A billion deadly worms engulf
a town in an orgy of horror!
Tonight's
8 O'Clock
Movie
56
WLVI
WITH FEWER
COMMERCIAL
INTERRUPTIONS

A MASTERPIECE OF SCIENCE FICTION
H.G.WELLS'
THE FOOD OF THE GODS
...for a taste of HELL!
MARJOE GORTNER
PAMELA FRANKLIN
RALPH MEEKER
JON CYPHER
IDA LUPINO
AND
THIS WAS THE NIGHT
of the Crawling Terror!
Squirm
an experience in PURE FRIGHT!!

www.ingramcontent.com/pod-product-compliance
Lightning Source LLC
Chambersburg PA
CBHW011144310726
48972CB00009B/2843